Over The Next Hill

Over The Next Hill

Gene R. Wilson

Dedicated to my beautiful wife, Judy, who took my words, fixed my spelling, and typed it up again, again and again.
Thank you for always believing in my dream.

All My Love, Your Gene

P.S. I Love You

ONE

The sound of hoofbeats on the trail leading to our ranch made me drop the hammer I was using to repair the barn door. Turning, I saw Dad's horse, Jake, running for the barn at a full gallop and was sure Pa was in bad trouble.

I grabbed her bridle as she flew by me headed for her stall. She was covered with sweat, and it took me several minutes to settle her down enough to get on her back. Her eyes rolled back in her head, and she snorted as froth sprayed from her mouth. I leaned over her dark neck and tried to calm her with sweet talk, but she was having none of that. I walked her for a few minutes, circling the ranch house. Finally, she let me head her down the south trail, the way she'd come.

Pa had gone to town this morning, riding Jake, a fine boned, strong bay. I felt sure I'd find sign of him along the trail. As I rode, noting each hoofprint as we crossed the shallow stream that cut through our ranch and loped across the green prairie, I felt the tension building. Pa could handle any horse. His gentle hand calmed many a frightened animal. No way would Pa leave a valuable horse like Jake to fend for herself. Either Pa sent Jake for help or Pa was in no condition to control Jake's movements.

About six miles down the trail all my fears were realized. There lay Pa, sprawled out in the dust with his head at a funny angle. His neck was broken.

The sign was plain as the nose on my face. Pa and I had tracked many deer, sometimes for meat, sometimes just for fun. I knew sign. A large cat had spooked the horse. It must have run right in front of Jake with a pack of wild dogs hot on the cougar's trail. Jake reared, going over backwards right on Pa.

Pa was dead, and me, a boy not quite fifteen, was left without a friend in the world. I sat there by the trail for what must have been several hours holding Pa's head in my lap sobbing like a three-year-old. All the pain of the last nine years rushed through my mind like a runaway stage.

First it was Ma taking sick with the fever and nothing we could do seemed to help. There were no doctors within a hundred miles of our campsite. We sat up all night covering her with cool, damp cloths every fifteen minutes, but it didn't help.

Just before dawn Pa gently placed her hands, one over the other, at her waist and kissed her, pulling the blanket over her face. Turning, he walked out into the night.

I stood there, not quite comprehending. As I stared at the still form under the blue patched cover I began to tremble.

Never again would she smile at me and take my hand as we tramped beside the wagon or tell me of those long, green hills back in Ohio filled with tall, straight trees and the family gatherings, loud and boisterous, overflowing with love and companionship.

I ran after Pa, crying, as I stumbled across the untraveled stretch of prairie. Pa held me, his own face dry and without expression as he said, "It's the Lord's wish."

I never quite accepted it the way Pa seemed to. Pa read the Good Book most every night. Maybe I was too young to have that much faith.

Little Becky was just barely walking when the Lord took her with the help of a rattlesnake. She loved to pick up rocks along the trail, filling her pockets and laid them in neat piles during the infrequent stops for repairs or meals. Neither Dad nor I saw or heard the rattler coiled in the shade of a pile of rocks left to mark the trail. It struck her small arm as she reached for a pebble lying close by. Dad literally flew to her side as she screamed, taking in the scene in one quick glance. As the snake slithered towards the rocks Pa grabbed those rattles and whipped it like an ox hide whip. I heard the sharp snap as the snake's neck broke.

Without a second glance Pa dropped the snake and ran to Becky. Her arm was swelling, and she cried something awful. Pa quickly pulled out his knife and asked me to hold Becky's arm tight. "Don't let her move, son."

I couldn't believe when he cut an X over the fang marks, all the time aware of the screams of my little sister. He lowered his head and sucked out the impure blood from her wound, spitting it off to the side. Repeating this many times he finally picked her up and gently held her to him, trying to comfort the frightened child.

Through the long hours as he held her, her small arm swelled to twice its size as her whimpering became lower and lower, until at long last she seemed to fall asleep. Only then did Pa tenderly Lay her on the rough floorboards of the covered wagon, wrapping her carefully in the tattered blanket she had so faithfully hugged to her chin each night.

Pa had trouble taking that. He just sat around and stared out into space for several days. Ma, and Becky, all in one year just about did Pa in.

I carefully lifted Pa over Jake's saddle and slowly walked those six long miles home to a now empty house full of memories.

I spent a sleepless night cleaning the cabin, each pot and bowl scoured and hanging in its place. I knew Pa wouldn't be happy if folks saw our cabin dirty.

Finally, I turned to Pa, knowing I must prepare him for his last trip to town. Carefully I ran his razor over the strap as I'd seen him do so many times. With trembling hands, I quickly shaved him, aware that he always looked neat when he went to town. I trimmed his curly dark hair and got out his best pair of jeans and the blue checkered shirt he favored. It took me a long time to get Pa dressed, but time didn't seem very important now.

It was just breaking light as I pulled the buckboard

around the front of our cabin. Taking our best blanket, the flowered one Ma was so proud of, I spread it on the wagon floor with a nice soft pillow for Pa's head. I was a big, strong boy but let me tell you, it was no easy chore getting Pa up in that wagon. I put a comforter over Pa, right up to his chin. Pa, he looked like he was asleep, except that his eyes were open. With tears coming down my cheeks we started off for Vandalia, nine miles away.

Stopping by the sheriff's office first, for I knew Sheriff Coy and Pa were good friends, I asked his help with the arrangements. The next day we buried Pa up on the hill next to Ma and Little Becky. It was drizzling rain which I thought fitting, for it seemed like even heaven was shedding a tear for Pa.

The town pretty well turned out for the funeral, for Pa, was well-liked. I thought I had spent all my tears, but when the Reverend Tomas started saying words over Pa-I cried like a baby.

After the funeral, Sheriff Coy took me aside and

asked what I planned to do. "I need a boy to sweep the office and do odd jobs around town," he offered.

"Thanks, Sheriff Coy, but the ranch holds a lot of sad memories and it's time for me to see what is on the other side of the hill."

Sheriff Coy set up the sale of the ranch to a family just moving west. It was a nice piece of land with abundant water and brought a good price. Ma had some fine pieces of furniture she insisted we bring from Ohio, and it hurt some for me to sell them, like the big oak hutch she polished every afternoon. Each nick and scratch had a special significance to a boy standing lonely and hurting as the pieces were hauled off.

All-totaled, farm, stock, and furniture I cleared one thousand, four hundred and seventy-eight dollars, more money than I thought existed.

The next morning, I put twelve hundred in the bank where I could draw off it when needed. Two hundred and seventy, I stuffed in my saddle bags, shook hands with Sheriff Coy and started west, not knowing where I was headed.

Jake was a good horse, for Pa was a breeder of fine horses. The saddle bags had food enough for a good week and my rifle would supply me with fresh game. The handgun felt strange on my side. I was a good shot with the rifle, but Pa never let me play with his sidearm. I carried two hundred rounds of forty-fours. I knew I needed to be alone for a while and let Jake have her head.

Two

That first evening I set up camp early, got my string and tin of hooks and went down by the brook to do some fishing. I do some of my best thinking that way. The water babbling over the rocks was just the medicine I needed. My hook found the calm, still water under an overhang and I just sat back enjoying the solitude. Suddenly the line jerked forward, heading for the opposite shore and rocks. I jerked the pole back and set the hooks, enjoying the give and take as slowly I pulled the bass in. A couple more like this one and I was in for a handsome feed. Fishing was good and grubs easy to find, so I didn't have to go into my packet of food except for salt. That fish sure tasted good. I believe it was the first meal I had since Pa died that didn't lump in my throat.

I sat there by the fire watching the stars

remembering the nights Pa and I sat on our front steps studying the formations in the dark sky. Pa knew some about their names and locations, Orion, the great hunter, Sirius, the dog star, and the North Star for directions. I spent many a night dreaming about those heavenly animals.

All the old memories started flooding through my mind. I was only five when Ma and Pa started west for Oregon. Little Becky was just crawling. I realize now from things Pa said that it was a disagreement with their kinfolk that started them west. Most folks went west to make a better life, but not so them. I remember Pa talking about the farm back in Ohio and it must have been grand, stretching for miles over rolling hills and meandering streams. They bred horses and I still recall the string of horses following our wagon. Then Ma took sick with the fever before we reached St. Louis. We buried her there in the town of Vandalia and Pa just couldn't go on and leave Ma behind. So, we bought a ranch just nine miles from town and every time Pa went to town he would stop and talk to Ma just like she could hear him.

Pa went to raising horses again, riding horses, gentle mares, prancing stallions and working cow ponies. Folks came from as far as St. Louis. Pa had been there once, about two years ago. I stayed home to tend stock, but Pa told me all about it when he got home.

He told of people from halfway around the world, all looking to start a new life, rough fur trappers, Orientals working on the railroad, wandering miners moving with each new rumor, slick gamblers and tough cattlemen all searching for a dream. He said wagon trains headed west almost every day filled with hard working men, strong women in homespun, excited kids and the tools to accomplish their visions: seeds, hoes, books, blankets, and memories of lives left in the dust of the wagons.

Shortly after noon I topped a hill overlooking the road to St. Louis. I just sat there not believing my eyes. I could see nine wagons coming down the road, people walking, women carrying children, goats, cows, and chickens in crates. Lots of men were carrying picks and shovels in one hand and a carpet bag and rifle in the other.

I rode Jake down and sort of blended in, asking one fellow where everyone was going.

"My word, boy! Haven't you heard! There's free land for the taking, plenty for everyone."

I let Jake have her head and just sat back and watched. Some of the wagons were so loaded down that the family had to walk alongside. The road had been traveled so much lately that some of the mud holes were two or three feet deep with ruts everywhere. Wagons continuously got stuck. Everyone pitched in and helped pull each other out, sometimes sinking into mud over their knees. I joined in and met some nice folks that way. They reminded me of Ma and Pa. It had to be rough on them, but I was having fun.

St. Louis lay across the river. I could see more

people right then than I'd ever seen. I wasn't sure I wanted to join them there on the muddy banks of the river. Folks said they had been lined up for days waiting for a turn on the ferry. There were several tents set up for gambling and whiskey flowed free.

That night I watched one man win three hundred dollars in one hand of poker. He was a small man and seemed to know cards. The gent across from him, a big man with a heavy black beard and cold, dark eyes, didn't like the way the cards were falling one bit. I decided right then I didn't know enough to play their game, but a fool and his money are soon parted.

When the dealer invited me to play, I told him truthfully, "I don't know how."

He laughed and said, "Son, you'll never learn any younger. Sit right down here and we'll teach you."

I lost five bucks in about two minutes. I had a lot to learn about poker. Telling them I was busted, I milled around for hours promising myself that one day I would learn these games of chance.

One of the bartenders grumbled, "Son, drink or gamble or get out!" My first taste of whiskey wasn't much better than my first attempt at gambling. I took a big swig like I saw the men at the bar doing, though the reaction was not quite like theirs. I coughed and half choked, spitting whiskey all over the place. It seemed to burn all the way down to my toes. Folks laughed and I laughed with them, but I had tears in my eyes.

"You guys really like this stuff?" I asked.

That started the laughter all over. It took a while, but I finally realized I had had more than my share of new experiences for the day, and I headed back to my camp.

THREE

I heard a ruckus back of the gambling tents. By the time I got there a crowd had gathered. There on the ground was the small man I saw win three hundred dollars the night before. His throat was cut from ear to ear. Talk was he had won more than nine hundred last night. All I could think of was those cold dark eyes staring at him across the battered table.

Before noon I heard of two more men that were hit on the head and robbed. Right then I made a point not to flash any money. I looked broke and should have no trouble.

After breakfast, I wandered down to the river. It sure was a long way to the other side. I threw a stick out a far piece to check the current. It was pretty fast, and I was sure it was worse out in the middle.

Two riders rode down the bank and started across. They seemed to go under and pop right back up. I watched closely, for I had it in my mind to do the same thing. They slid off their horses and grabbed the saddle horns and let the horses do the work. The river was taking them downstream fast, so I ran along the bank to keep an eye on them. A tree came downstream just missing the second horse. I could just imagine what would have happened had the tree and the horse tangled out there. Both riders made it but were far downstream and seemed to have trouble getting up the other bank.

I made up my mind I wasn't about to walt around here for four or five days for no old ferry. If those guys could do it, so could I. I put my gun and holster in the saddlebags along with my skinning knife, wrapped my ammo in oil shin, tied my saddle gun in place and made sure my bedroll would stay on and I was off to face the river.

I looked upstream as far as I could see for floating

trees before I urged Jake down the bank. I could tell she wasn't too keen on the idea. We were almost halfway when I saw a large branch rolling and coming straight at us. I tried to turn Jake downstream but couldn't reach the reins. The tree hit us with a terrible impact. Jake's hind leg hit me and sent me down. I could feel branches hitting me and spinning me around now. My lungs seemed to be bursting for air and still, I was under water.

Finally, my head popped up. Gasping for air I looked around for Jake, she was nowhere in sight. The tree was two hundred feet downstream from me, but I couldn't see Jake. I pulled off my boots and let them go, for I knew I had no chance to make shore with them on. I had been swimming for about ten minutes when a dead log came by, and it surely saved my life. I grabbed hold and sort of rested, kicking my feet to steer it to the opposite shore.

When my feet scraped bottom, I let go of the log and stumbled up the bank. I lay there breathing hard more from fright than from the strain. That was my first brush with death.

The stones hurt my feet as I walked downstream looking for Jake.

She must have got tangled in the tree for I looked until dark and found no sign of her. I sat on the bank thinking about the mess I got myself in. No horse, gun, knife, blanket of food and no boots I sure did it up this time. Would I ever learn patience? I couldn't wait the five days for the ferry. What hurt the worst was to lose a good horse and Jake was one of the best.

I woke up with the sun in my eyes and my belly growling for I hadn't eaten since breakfast yesterday. There grazing quietly a few feet from me was Jake with a large bruise on her hind quarter where the tree had hit her. A lost shoe had her limping too. I hugged her neck and cried a little, my last link with home.

Jake and I walked the ten or twelve miles upstream to St. Louis on some very tender feet. It was late afternoon when I reached town and set myself down for a good meal. I had to show them I had the price of a meal before they would serve me. I can't say I blamed them much for I must have looked a sight. My pants were torn, one sleeve was missing from my shirt, and I had no boots. It cost me a dollar and a half for that supper, and I made up my mind if I were to stay in this town very long, I was going to have to find a job.

A visit to the general store soon had me looking respectable once more and I began to canvas the businesses looking for work.

Half the people in town must have had the same idea.

As I passed the blacksmith, a horse waiting to be shoed, nervous, and high string, began to shift and stomp. Remembering Pa's gentle hand, I quietly and quickly grabbed his bridle firmly, holding his head down and whispered a string of low words calming the horse. The blacksmith worked quickly, finishing the small mare and turned her over to her owner.

I led the tall Appaloosa to the smithy. "Sir, you need an extra hand. I know horses and need a job."

He chuckled and said, "I believe you're right. My name's Dan Lang, young fella." and he extended his large muscular hand. "Put a little muscle on that lanky frame, and I'll soon have me a partner. If you stay at least six months, I'll teach you the trade." He offered.

"Mr. Lang," I answered truthfully, "I can't guarantee any length of time. There are too many hills I haven't seen behind yet. But I helped my Pa back home some and know a little about shoeing."

Mr. Lang laughed and said, "I was young once myself and felt the same way."

So, we struck a bargain. Mr. Lang and I became good friends, and he insisted I have my meals with him and his missus. I was getting paid seventy-five cents a day, plus free meals. Sleeping in the stable I soon saved the money back I had to spend on new boots and clothes.

FOUR

One thing about working at a blacksmith and livery stable, you don't miss much that is going on around town. I was kind of a hero when some of the old timers found I could read, a bit slow and occasionally stumbling over words, but able to read them. They brought me the St. Louis Weekly and the infrequent letter some of them received from families back east and I would read to them when I was caught up with my work. In return they would tell me stories of the places they had seen and the characters they'd met.

Old Mort had been a trapper when the French were first traveling the river. He told me about Jean LaPorte and his flat boats plying the river, bringing in a fortune in furs. Once he shared a drink with Mr. Love, the wagon master who opened the Love Trail down New Mexico way. We sat in the sunshine and studied the flow of travelers passing through this Gateway to the West. Mort pointed out all the ways these people protected themselves.

"Watch for a knife in the boots of those riverboat men. They're swift and accurate." he warned me as we watched the passengers disembark from the fancy riverboats.

"Notice the bulge under the shoulder of that gambler? A pistol for sure. And that little lady whose purse looks a mite heavy, look out for her.

As a crowd of boisterous, rowdy men passed by, Mort pointed to one of the louder, mean looking cowboys and quietly told me, "Now that big brawny fellow, no gun, but watch out for his fists and keep an eye out for that holster hung low on the hip too. That fellow knows how to handle a gun, and it's probably fast too!"

"By the way, if you intend to keep wearing that gun of your Pa's you had better know how to use it."

I watched and listened and grew to know the characters, the loud mouths looking for trouble and the quiet dangerous ones. Out behind a low hill Mort and I set up targets. With my rifle I was a sure shot, but I still shied away from Pa's handgun, missing the cans more than hitting them.

And so, the winter passed. My six months with Mr. Lang were just about up. It was time to look for more hill's further west.

One day a young man walked into the stable and said, "Son, I want to rent a horse."

The stranger was dressed fit to kill. His boots were almost new, shined so you could see your face in them. The dark pants he wore had a crease down the front and were made of fine wool and his white shirt had ruffles at the sleeves and down the front. The vest under his jacket was a silky green material and his fawn jacket hung open. It fits like a glove. He wore a string tie with a turquoise stone set in gold. His hat was felt with a broad rim and almost snow white. The holster had silver trim and the gun in it sported a pearl handle. When his coat swung open, I could see he also had a small handgun in some sort of shoulder rig. The handle was also pearl.

To a farm boy like me used to homespun he looked like a king, but his clothes marked him as a gambler.

"My name's Cobb. Most folks call me T.J." he explained as he reached out his hand.

I shook his hand and said, "My name is Jimmy. What sort of horse are you looking for, Mr. Cobb?"

He laughed and said, "The best you got, son, the best you got!"

I showed him three of our best horses, telling him the palomino was quite a looker, but if he wanted staying power, I suggested the big roan. The mustang was by far the most trail wise for it was mountain bred.

He settled on the mustang saying, "You never know when you might need a good horse under you."

Saddling him T.J. asked where he could find some

good fishing. A boy of fifteen always knows the best spots. I sent him down the stream several miles where there was a bend in the river and a log snagged halfway across. I'd caught my supper there many a day.

In the weeks that followed T.J. and I became good friends. We went on several fishing trips together. He was a gambler and had been working the river between St. Louis and New Orleans. During the winter he worked a table at the Silver Spur.

Many evenings I would go over and watch him deal blackjack. He always had lots of players for no doubt his game was straight. In the days that followed he taught the art of dealing to me.

I spent hours memorizing the order the cards would fall. Even though the deck was well shuffled, many cards would fall in the same order as the time before.

He had me roll a coin back and forth across my fingers to loosen them up and make them limber.

"No gambler can make a living without a good

memory and limber fingers," T.J. taught.

I practiced by the hour. Soon my fingers did things unconsciously.

Instinctively my fingers reached for a coin anytime I was standing idle.

Next, he taught me how to see things with my mind. He would put several items on a board and cover them with a cloth, flash the cover back and quickly recover them. Then he would ask what I saw. At first, I remembered very little, but as he worked with me, I saw more and more. Soon I could identify twenty or more items with just a flash look.

One day he asked if I could use the sidearm, I carried. I told him, "I'm a crack shot with a rifle, but the handgun was Pa's and I had only shot it a couple of times without much success." "Well, Jimmy, if you're going to carry it you best learn how to use it, for someday someone will surely challenge you."

After looking over Pa's gun he suggested I purchase

a new one if I could afford it. The next morning T.J and I went gun shopping. We settled on a new model Colt had just manufactured. The action was smooth, and it seemed to jump out of the new holster. I couldn't wait to practice with it. T.J. told me not to hurry it out of the holster for that would come with practice, just concentrate on hitting what I aimed at.

"It don't matter how fast you are, if you can't hit what you're aiming at." T.J. insisted.

It seemed I was a natural, for as the weeks went by my aim was true and my speed increased. I hardly had time to sleep, what with tending horses during the day, practicing out back with my six shooter until dark and then working with T.J. until the tables shut down for the night. Every place I went I practiced with the coin running up and down my fingers. I even took up juggling to help my coordination. Mort got a good laugh out of that.

Finally, one warm day in early May T.J. stopped by,

saying, "It's time to hit the river again."

T.J. was like an older brother that I never had, and he could see the hurt in my eyes as he spoke.

"Hey Jimmy, what say you come along? I'll work the poker game and you can run a small blackjack table."

The next day I talked it over with the Langs. They had been as close to parents as I was going to find. They wanted me to stay but understood my need to move on. Missus Lang invited T.J and I to one last home cooked meal. Her fried chicken reminded me of Ma's. The biscuits dripped with honey and were followed with fresh apple pie topped with heavy cream. We pushed back from the table and loosened our belts. I was going to miss the Lang's.

Mr. Lang bought Jake from me with the understanding that if I came back this way, I could buy her back.

"By the way, Jimmy, how does a mare come by the name Jake?"

Mr. Lang asked me as he led her back to her stall.

I laughed and explained, "I was just a little feller. It was the first colt born after we lost Ma and Pa said I could name it. I liked Jake, so it stood. I've been teased a mite about it."

FIVE

The paddle boat was scheduled to leave shortly after noon, but T.J. said, "No riverboat gambler worth a two-bit bet, ever wore blue jeans and flannel. Come on, we've got some shopping to do."

T.J. outfitted me to look just like him, tight pants, white ruffled shirt, and fawn jacket. The only difference was the shoulder holster for he said that would get me into more trouble than I could get myself out of. I had gained a lot of muscle over the winter just as Mr. Lang promised and had to strain to get the trousers over my large thighs. I felt kind of strange in the tight-fitting clothes favored by riverboat men but strutted just the same.

And boy, was I proud as we walked down the street and waved to Mort sitting with his cronies on the boardwalk. My carpet bag held two more sets of clothes, plus Pa's old forty-four. I still had almost as much money in my pocket as I had started off with. That would be my bank to start the blackjack table.

"You have to pay the captain ten dollars each night for the table, win or lose." T.J. explained to me.

I was excited as we approached the gangplank for, I had never seen one up close, let alone rode on it. It was the most beautiful paddle boat I'd ever seen, though truth be known it was the only one I'd ever seen. Gingerbread woodwork covered the upper deck, and the main saloon was beyond anything I'd ever dreamt of, all red plush carpeting, polished brass everywhere and woodwork rubbed to a glowing sheen.

I looked back on St. Louis with fond memories for I had made some good friends. Old Mort and his stories would see me through many a quiet evening under the stars and I would surely miss the Lang's. Mr. Lang had been good to me and taught me a lot in the eight short months I stayed with them. In an emergency I could always fall back on the blacksmith trade, but now I was starting a new page in my life.

The steward showed T.J. and I, our room. It had six bunks in it, three on a side. Me, being the smallest, and the youngest, got the top bunk. T.J. took the middle one on the same side. I crawled up to try mine and was surprised how little room there was, but I spent so little time there it hardly mattered. Four others drifted in, throwing their bags on the empty bunks, and headed for the bar.

Later the steward stopped in and growled, "Tables open at eight and close at two." and collected the first night's fee.

T. J. was an old hand at this and gave me some last-minute tips, plus had me run the inevitable coin through my fingers to loosen me up. As the clock approached eight, I opened the door and stepped out on the deck, ready to face my first night as a gambler. I took a deep breath and followed T.J. into the saloon.

My table opened right at eight and you could hear a buzz go through the crowd when they saw a boy running a table. The first couple of hours I was just holding my own. Then the butterflies went away. I began to relax and enjoy myself, remembering all the tips T.J. had taught me. I started talking more and the cards turned my way. The next three hours I could do no wrong. I wound up winning one hundred sixty-three dollars on my very first night.

At two o'clock I strolled out to the stern, checked that no one was listening and gave out with a great "Yahoooo!"

Play was extremely heavy at my table the first few evenings for everyone thought they could beat the kid. I had some bad nights too, for the cards run funny at times. T.J. laughed one night when I told him I lost three hundred dollars.

He reminded me, "That's good for business."

I settled into my new life and was really enjoying it,

for this was an adventure to a sixteen-year-old, my birthday passing unnoticed while I dealt cards.

When the boat stopped at small towns to take on wood, T.J. and I would visit the local gambling places. First, we would change our clothes so that we didn't look like ringers. I learned how to play poker that way. My memory was excellent. That helped with the game and soon I was relieving dealers at the poker tables as we headed for New Orleans.

One evening enjoying a game in one of the small towns I saw the dealer slip a card from the bottom, but as I was money ahead, I just begged out of the game rather than start trouble in a strange town.

Later T.J. said I did the right thing. The last thing a gambler needs is that kind of trouble as I was soon to learn.

We had been on the river for about nine weeks when three trappers came on board, loud and pushy. T.J. took one look and told me to watch myself for they were bad news. Poker was their game so that left my table free and believe me, I was glad. While they traveled with us, I stuck to blackjack.

Two nights later the two of them sat down at T.J.'s table and started playing buddies. When one of them had a good hand, he would signal the other to raise the ante and try to get someone in the middle feeding the pot. They were good but drank too much. Finally, they got T.J. in the middle. One would raise, then the other. At the end of the hand the one called Pete turned over three aces and two threes and started to rake in the pot.

T.J. turned over four sevens and said, "Looks like you lose."

For a moment you could hear a pin drop. Pet yelled, "You cheated." and went for his gun.

T.J. just seemed to sit there, and I knew he was dead. There was nothing I could do. Two shots sounded, one after another and Pete slumped over on the floor with two holes in his chest. n T.J.'s left hand was a small sleeve gun that appeared out of nowhere. The tables closed for the night.

Early the next morning the captain woke us. "You're bad for business. We'll be in Commerce in a couple of hours. I want you off." We stood on the dock, carpetbags in hand, watching the boat steam down the river. Another, smaller and much slower one was due in a couple hours.

My profits were over two thousand dollars for five weeks' work.

T.J. wanted to catch the next boat, but I was yearning for the blue skies and green hills without smoke and closed-in rooms. Fall was fast approaching, and I wanted to breathe the cool, crisp air.

It hurt plenty to say goodbye to T.J. for he was truly a friend, but a new hill was beckoning. We parted on the dock. My last glimpse of T.J. was a tall gambling man casually leaning on the railing, slowly flipping the inevitable coin through his fingers.

SIX

We both had a way to go, and time was passing. I turned and walked into town. First, I needed to get the feel of the town and my slick clothes would be a hindrance. I ducked down an alley behind some crates to make a quick change, set my carpet bag down next to my rifle and started to strip.

Just as I slipped off my pants two boys turned into the alley. Quickly I pulled on my jeans and buttoned them. Dressed in bib overalls, shirtless and barefoot, the taller of the two stretched out his hand as though to shake hands and I reached out mine. His left fist hit me hard in the left cheek and blood ran in my mouth. I reached for my face as his right caught me in the stomach and doubled me over. Grabbing my hair, he pulled my head down as his knee came smashing up into my nose. Blood splattered down my white shirt.

"Leave him to me. He's all mine." I heard as I staggered backward.

Two more jabs to the face and I was still on my feet. I hit the wall and bounced back right into a solid punch to the stomach. Doubled over I went down, and he stepped back, giving me room to get up. Slowly I pulled myself up. He came in again, with a series of jabs to the body. I never even got one punch in. This time I went down and stayed down, never completely losing consciousness. That's when the younger of the two kicked me three or four times in the ribs.

Somewhere in the distance a bell sounded, a dinner bell. The angel Gabriel could not have been more welcome.

"Ma will shin us if we're late for supper again. Let's go. He knows who runs this town now." They walked out of the alley leaving me lying there in the dust and my own blood.

I laid there for several minutes heaving, trying to

get my breath after the blows to my stomach. I rolled over, tasting the blood in my mouth and felt like throwing up. Leaning against the wall for a few minutes I pulled off what was left of my fancy white shirt and held it against my face.

T.J. had taught me a lot of things, but he hadn't covered fist fighting. I would learn if I was to survive out here. It had happened so quickly I didn't know what happened. Even if I had, the end result would have been the same.

They had been so busy kicking and smacking me they never noticed my carpet bag and rifle. My jacket lay folded neatly over a crate where I laid it just before they descended on me.

I stumbled to my bag and pulled out my flannel shirt. At least I looked respectable enough to pass inspection as I carefully stepped out of the alley and walked forty agonizing feet to the local hotel, a two story, ramshackle building, not long for this town.

For an extra two bits the graying, unshaven agent brought up a pitcher of lukewarm water grumbling the whole way about extra work.

Carefully I washed and rinsed my battered body, knowing tomorrow I'd be one mass of bruises. Rest was what I needed now as I lowered my body to the sagging mattress. A feather bed never felt better, and I slept around the clock.

Rising with the sun in my eyes I slowly changed clothes and attempted a quick wash-up and wandered down to the street looking for a hot meal.

It didn't take long to realize this was not the town for me. Going into the Blue Bull I had to step over a drunk asleep on the steps. Inside the saloon the room reeked of stale beer. The bar, a board laid across two kegs, had never seen soap and water. An argument erupted between two of the scruffier customers. When they started trading punches and fell out the door I followed and walked off in another direction.

The only restaurant besides the bar was not much better. The tables were dirty and what food I could see through the dingy window was greasy. I could do better beside my own campfire, but I needed a horse. So, I made my way down to the livery, a crude barn in need of repair and ambled through a door hanging from one rusty hinge.

Inside, a young boy was attempting to clean stalls. From the stench in the barn, he was going to be busy for a long time.

"Looks like you have a mighty big job in front of you." I commented. "How about I trade you some help for information."

Tim knew a good deal when he heard it. The two of us shoveled and spread fresh straw for three hours. It kind of felt good after spending nine weeks mostly sitting in smoke filled gambling rooms and my battered body needed to work out the kinks.

In between, Tim told how he lost his family in a flash prairie fire. He had gone downstream a ways to catch some supper and had time only to duck under the water as the fire roared over his head. He crawled out to a scene of desolation, gray ashes everywhere. Walking back to camp he found the burned forms of his two sisters, ma, and pa. They never had a chance. The wagon was unhitched. They had run about twenty feet. There on the prairie he buried them, leaving the oxen where they fell. A boy can only do so much.

And here he walked, to this dying river town, taking any job to keep food in his stomach and a place to sleep.

His family was heading for Denver where his father was going into partnership with an old friend in the newspaper business. Tim's father knew how to keep those clanking, ink-covered machines putting out clean copy.

I needed a good solid horse with staying power and Tim suggested I try old man Henson's place.

I rented us both horses from the livery and rode out. Mr. Henson's was the only thing I'd seen in this river town worth remembering. Inside a well-built corral was a mixed herd of gentle riding mares, cowboy ponies and wild mustangs. What a beautiful sight it was to see spirited well-kept horse flesh again. A spotted mustang with a proud way of carrying himself caught my eye. Mr. Henson threw in an old saddle, and I had me a horse.

Tim and I spent the night around my campfire swapping stories about our childhood. I told him about my initiation to this river-boat town. "That had to be John and Tom Burrows. They wander around town like they own it, looking for trouble and anyone they can bully. I mostly stayed out of their way."

By morning I knew I couldn't leave Tim in this broken-spirited town, but he didn't have the wandering urge that grew inside of me.

"Tim," I said, "You need to follow your Pa's trail. Someone in Denver is waiting for the Wordel family. What say I stake you to a stagecoach ticket to Denver. There you can locate your Pa's partner and begin a life for yourself. This town will be gone in another year."

Mid-morning found us headed for Scott City, the nearest town on the stagecoach line. Tim had me print my name clear on the margin of an ace of diamonds from a ragged deck he carried in his pocket to pass the time.

"The next time you're in Denver your money will be waiting for you with the ace of diamonds on top. Just ask for Tim Wordel and the nearest newspaper." Tim said as he shook my hand and stepped aboard the stage.

It felt mighty good to use money squandered in a poker game for the benefit of what looked to be a solid citizen of some western town.

SEVEN

I let Lance set the pace the next morning and was almost asleep in the saddle when he snorted. Instantly awake I straightened in the saddle just as I heard the crack of a rifle and a burning in my shoulder. As I fell off backwards, I realized I'd been shot. I fell on my belly. Pulling my six gun, I cocked the hammer and lay still for I didn't know where the shot had come from. My pony stopped about thirty feet in front of me. I lay there watching him, unable to reach cover and listened as the riders pulled up, two of them.

"Hell, Sam, it's just a kid. He won't have any money."

"Morely, check his saddle bags while I go through his pockets."

I could see the one called Morely as he got off his

horse. He holstered his gun and, force of habit, he put the thong over the hammer.

Sam was coming from behind me. I could hear the creak of the saddle as he got off. I rolled over with my gun in hand. He still had his gun in his hand but pointed down. I aimed straight for his chest, but he turned, and my bullet caught his shooting arm just above the elbow. He screamed and dropped his gun.

I swung my gun towards Morely who was trying to draw his, but the thong kept it in place. He raised his hands and that saved his life for I was pulling back on the trigger.

Sam lay on the ground, clutching his shattered arm. "Morely, get over there next to your partner where I can keep an eye on both of you." I snarled. "Drop your gun belt with your left hand."

My voice sounded strange, and I realized I was trembling. Now my shoulder was beginning to throb, and I could feel blood running down the inside of my shirt.

What was I going to do with them? It was a four hard day's ride back to the river town. Sam was complaining about his arm, and it had to be hurting something awful as bad as it looked. I tied Morely's hands behind his back and went through their saddlebags. I found two bottles of whiskey. Pulling my shirt off I saw that their bullet had burned across the top of my shoulder, hurting, but not serious. I poured whiskey on it, and it burned like hell. I enjoyed pouring whiskey on Sam's arm for I knew how it had to hurt and wrapped his arm the best I could in my white dress shirt.

When Sam realized I was not about to let them go, he told me about a trading post two hours north of here. I checked the ropes on Morely, emptied their rifles and hung their holsters over my saddle horn and we were off, with Sam in the lead and me bringing up the rear.

The trading post was a small settlement consisting of the trading post, a blacksmith shop, and a tavern with five horses standing at the rail. As we rode up to the trading post a man with a long bushy beard stepped out, his rifle held low but ready.

"Howdy, young fellow." was his greeting. "What can I do for you?"

"I'm looking for the law." I stated simply.

"Ain't no law around here, mister. What them fellers done?"

"They tried to bushwhack me down the trail. You got a doc in these parts?" I asked.

"Nope. Mary, over at the tavern, can fix you up. What she can't handle we take over to Bob at the blacksmith shop. He doubles as our undertaker. Got a big tree out back if you want to hang 'um. Need help, just give a yell. We'll be glad to. Been purty quiet around here. I'll give you a fair price for their guns. "

We rode on down to the saloon. I could see fear in Morely's eyes for the first time. Mary was a large woman with a pleasant face. She wore a calico dress with a big apron over it.

She smiled and said, "Looks like you had a mite of trouble, son."

I told her what had happened.

She checked Sam's shoulder. "That arm looks pretty bad, but we can keep the infection down." she commented as she led us inside. "You'll never be able to use it again, at least not for bushwhacking."

I asked Mary's husband to keep an eye on the two desperados and went over to the trading post to sell their guns. Mary was finishing up Sam as I walked in. She took a look at my shoulder, noting the bruises covering my shoulder and back and gave me some salve to use. As she finished bandaging my shoulder, I handed her the sixty dollars I'd gotten for their guns.

"I can't take all of this." she said.

But when I explained where the money came from, she smiled and thanked me. With only the stage stop bringing in extra money this unexpected bounty would be put to good use.

Turning to Sam and Morely I snapped, "If I ever see you again, I'll shoot on sight. You have ten minutes to ride out of town before I change my mind and hang you."

They started to protest, insisting they needed their guns for food and protection, but one look at the smithy standing off to the side playing with a rope and they stomped out within five minutes.

I stayed the night, enjoying a home cooked meal under a roof and agreeable conversation to boot.

Mary fed me a breakfast of potatoes and eggs with a steak on the side and thick black coffee. I'd ride a long way on that meal. After I bought a couple cans of peaches, some beans, onions, salt, and flour and thanked them for their hospitality I headed west.

EIGHT

In the days that followed I found I really got a bargain when I bought Lance. He had already saved my life back there when he snorted, but he was also sure-footed and found water more than once for me. I soon learned to trust his judgment. If he headed off, I let him have his head for he would surely find water.

One chilly morning a wild boar, evidently some farmer's loss, came charging out of the brush. My hand drew almost automatically, and my aim was true. A silver dollar could have covered the two bullet holes. I stuffed myself that night for it had been a long time since I had any kind of pork.

A week passed as I built a small smokehouse, butchered the hog, and smoked the fresh pork. Now I had bacon and fat back to last a good while.

My mind and body needed time to rest, to revive and the miles slipped by as Lance, and I enjoyed the solitude.

It had been over a month since I left the settlement without seeing a single person when I heard the cows. At first, I thought it might be a small herd of strays, but as I rode over the top of the ridge, there were, before me, more cattle than I'd ever seen in one bunch. They were four or five abreast and strung out for half a mile or more. I counted six cowboys, plus a chuck wagon and a remuda of horses. I followed alongside the herd until they made camp.

Hailing the camp, I rode in. Cookie had the meal started in record time and invited me to have a cup of coffee, while I waited for the boys to come in. They got the herd settled and started drifting in. The trail boss was a rangy man in his late thirties.

I took a liking to him right away and I guess he liked what he saw as he extended his hand, introduced himself as Johnson and said they could use an extra hand if I was looking for work.

"I'm heading west, but in no hurry." I explained as we sat around the fire.

"The pay is a dollar fifty per day, paid when we pull into Abilene."

I teamed up with a cowboy called Rover. Rover was probably the oldest of the lot and mighty trail wise. He was good with a lasso and in a few days was teaching me how to handle the rope. Soon I had a working knowledge of the lasso, but I'd never win any prizes with it. In the days that followed I learned a lot about cattle, mostly how dumb and stubborn they can be.

As low man on the totem pole, I mostly rode drag catching all the dust and stink two thousand cows can make. We had a couple troublemakers that broke every chance they got, but the old mossback that led the herd was worth his weight in gold for he kept the herd moving at a good pace.

We hit one stretch without water for six days. Covered with a fine dust from morning to night that crept into our food, bedrolls, and guns, we grumbled as each night we reoiled our guns.

Cowboys without their morning coffee would not endear themselves to anyone. The herd was restless, and we worried about a stampede. The night guard was doubled, and tempers were growing short.

The next morning the old mossback smelled water and the herd was off to the races. All we could do was stay out of their way and hope we wouldn't lose too many at the river when they bunched and fought for access to the water.

In two hours, they covered twelve miles and there we found them, strung out, placidly drinking water. Johnson decided to hold the herd there for a couple days. We all needed to soak up some of that water and the cattle needed a little fattening up after their run.

Extra shirts, kerchiefs and jeans hung from low

branches and bushes as we shook the dust from our gear. We played in the river like a bunch of boys at the local swimming hole, dunking the unaware and splashing water in all directions. For several days we soaked up water and the cattle peacefully grazed nearby.

I won a place for myself on that drive when I came back to camp with ten nice catfish. Cookie outdid himself that night and we all relaxed around the fire, singing songs from home, and telling tales of old heroes and live legends. I took it all in, dust and all, and loved every minute of it, warm days, cool nights, and long evenings around the fire.

The next two weeks were fun for a sixteen-year-old. Of course, I was the youngest and least experienced, but the river crossings were exciting. Cookie did a lot of cussing every time he saw one. All his dry goods had to be stored above the floor of the chuck wagon and the pots and pans tied tightly to the sides so that they wouldn't float away. The cows lowed all the way across, trying to climb over the back of the one in front, until the opposite bank was a mass of sloppy mud two feet thick.

The mountains came into view days before we got close to them. Johnson rode off each morning looking for a pass accessible to the cattle. There was only one way. But it seemed a man named Collins set claim to the pass and charged a duty for each man, horse, and cow to use it and he had four hard cases to back his play. Johnson told us the situation saying Collins wanted two hundred dollars or ten percent of the cattle.

"I think we could get through, but I'm afraid we'll lose part of the herd and some good men. It's two hundred miles around and I don't have the money to pay so the only thing left is to let them cut the herd." Johnson explained.

He walked away, his head down, twisting the problem around in his head, trying to come up with a better solution.

The boys and I just kind of milled around with our coffee, not knowing how we could help, willing to make a run for it, but not looking forward to a bullet finding us.

After dark Baler, the best tracker on the drive, slipped through their defenses and studied the stronghold. High boulders rimmed the narrow trail through the pass, wide enough for three or four cows' shoulder to shoulder. From the boulders two or three men could hold back an army brigade, shooting anyone with other ideas.

This unwelcome news Baler brought back as we sat dejected around the fire.

Maybe I could help. I got Johnson off to the side and told him I had the money he needed if he wanted it. He could pay me back when he sold the herd. Johnson didn't question why a sixteen-year-old was riding with that much money in his pocket and jumped at the offer, better than losing men or cattle.

The next day Johnson parleyed with Collins. From the set of his back, you could see he was holding back a powerful urge to knock Collins flat on his back and take his chances. As we drove the herd through the pass, we could see we'd have been cut down like fish in a bowl. They just sat up in the rocks, their guns across their knees and watched us pass. Just as easily they could have picked us off one by one and no one the wiser. We all rode easier when the last cow passed through the pass.

The rest of the journey went uneventful, and we pulled into Abilene dust covered, dirty and ready to enjoy civilization again. We held the cattle out of town a few miles while Johnson went in to make a deal with the cattle buyers. Since we were one of the last herds to get through before winter set in, prices were high.

We brought the cattle into the holding pens and Johnson paid us off with a ten-dollar bonus. He thanked me for the loan and offered to buy me a drink. I told him I'd meet him later at the saloon.

I left Johnson at the pens watching the count and rode down to the bars whooping and yelling with the rest of the boys. It had been a good many weeks since any of us were able to blow off any steam. The town was wide open to the cattlemen as long as they stayed on the right side of the tracks and didn't get too carried away. We hit one bar after another. The whiskey still burned going down and I switched to beer.

Johnson caught up to us in the Silver Slipper, one of the better drinking establishments west of the Mississippi. They had games of chance that I had never seen before and had to try. The dance hall girls dressed in bright reds, brilliant greens, and vivid oranges like the sunset. In one corner a man played the piano. I remembered seeing one back in Ohio when I was just a squirt. I was all eyes and a bit green around the edges as far as the girls were concerned.

At eight o'clock there would be a stage show featuring Miss Lily and if she was half as pretty as the painting showed, I for one, was not going to miss it.

All the dealers dressed much like I had on the riverboat, shuffling cards under a high ceiling dotted with shimmering chandeliers. Coal oil lamps hung from the walls cast a rich glow over the scene. I could see how a cowboy would brag about losing his money in this kind of atmosphere and enjoy it.

Johnson and I went into the dining room and ordered steaks. We were served on real China with the thinnest glasses I'd ever held, and the silverware looked to be gold. The meal was one of the best I'd ever had, but I thought they would never get it all out to us. They brought one thing at a time. I'd have liked to wolf it all down at once, but a glance around showed others slowly eating, talking, and enjoying themselves. So, I just set myself back and tried to act the gentleman. They brought us a salad, waited until we were both done, which wasn't long in my case, took the empty plates and replaced them with vegetable soup. I noticed no one lifted the bowl and drank so I carefully dipped it out spoon by spoon, slower but effective.

Then they brought out a juicy steak that covered

the plate, fresh green beans, plus a baked potato and lots of butter. Johnson begged off when dessert was offered but I was a growing boy, so I had fresh berry pie with ice cream.

Again, I remembered home, Pa stirring up the milk and sugar to make us ice cream. It took ages, but he would let me sample every couple of minutes and Ma, looking pretty, smiled as she scooped out a bowl for each of us. It seemed so long ago.

Johnson offered me a partnership if I would go back to Texas with him and bring another herd north before the northers started blowing.

It was tempting, but I wanted to head west not south. So, Johnson picked up the tab for the meal and set off to do some drinking of his own.

I wanted to try my luck at the gaming tables before the show started. I had almost four hundred dollars in my pockets, and it was burning a hole.

I lost pretty near fifty dollars before the show

started. My head was a little fuzzy and I vaguely remembered T.J. saying something about not mixing cards and liquor. But the show was worth fifty dollars. Miss Lily was the most beautiful creature I'd seen since Ma, though she was painted up a bit too much for my tastes. Her dress was full and made a pretty sound as she danced across the stage. And then she started to sing. The men yelled requests and she sang of lost loves, prairie land, wagon trains and folks back home. I felt tears coming and looking sideways to hide them saw several others trying to wipe their eyes unobserved. We kept her up there for two hours clapping and yelling our heads off.

NINE

I stayed in town for almost two weeks, having the time of my life. When I finally left my jeans were much lighter, for I had only seventeen dollars left, but no regrets.

The next several weeks I lived off the land, hunting for my supper or catching fish. They were good days, and I was enjoying myself. My pony seemed to enjoy the lazy days too, for I had pushed him hard on the cattle drive and then neglected him in the livery stable. If I didn't wake up at the crack of dawn Lance would trot over to my bedroll and give me a nudge. We were becoming best friends and depended on each other.

The further west we went the more scarce game became. I had to eat out of my saddlebags for the last four days. The country was rolling plains with grass up to Lance's knees, so he was having no problems.

The ground was covered with frost as I rolled out of my bedroll, and I skipped breakfast for an early start sure I would see an antelope or deer. The frost was heavy and if anything moved across the prairie it would leave a trail a blind man could follow.

As I topped a little knoll I caught sight of tracks about two hundred yards off to my left.

I could see where more than one something had crossed through the small valley, but as I sat there studying the trail something didn't feel right. Suddenly the hair came up on the back of my neck as I realized what was wrong. I was not alone. Those were tracks left by people, for no animal would go that far in a straight line. I reached in my saddle bags, pulled out the spyglass and looked the country over. Nothing stirred but I realized this rolling country could hide a small army. I loosened the thong on my hammer just in case and studied Lance to see if I had missed any reaction, but he seemed very calm.

I'd watch him closely for he would sense something before me, I was sure.

After a few minutes I walked Lance down to the fresh trail to study the tracks. They were strange, for I could see people were walking, but there were no heel marks, led by one horse with no shoes and limping on the left front leg. Two straight lines followed the horse, cutting in deep, first on one side then the other.

I could see where one of the people had fallen down, with no visible reason for him falling. I found no traces of blood though I thought he might be hurt. Deciding to backtrack them to their camp to see what I could learn I was surprised that they never went more than five hundred yards without stopping to rest. Now I wondered if possibly they were sick instead of hurt. I still hadn't found one boot mark.

Their camp was only about a mile from where I first

spotted the tracks. The coals were barely warm, so I knew they had broken camp early and were moving very slowly. Of course, I should have realized it immediately, they were all wearing moccasins. One of them had a bad foot for one foot made tracks at a right angle. It wasn't bothering him as he didn't seem to favor it. At least two appeared to be women.

As slow as they traveled, I decided it would be safe to get a closer look at them. I could study them from more than a mile off with my glass. I started back down their trail but didn't follow right behind them. Instead, I stayed a couple hundred feet off to the side of the trail. It was easy to follow, for whatever they were pulling, knocked the grass down two feet wide.

I was surprised how fast I caught up to them. Riding over a rolling hill there they were not five hundred yards from me. They saw me immediately. So, I just sat my horse and looked them over with my glass. To my surprise they were old.

I thought out loud, "No wonder they traveled so slow. The one with the bad foot is the only young person among the lot."

I counted four old men, two old women and a young cripple of about thirteen, with a pony that looked half dead pulling a large load on a travois made of two poles and an animal skin pulled taut across it.

They watched me for a while and when I made no move towards them, they started moving again. I just sat my horse and watched them.

That evening, I came upon a small herd of buffalo, I pulled my rifle up, took careful aim and killed a half-grown calf. The rest of the herd just stood there looking at me. They didn't start running until I tramped down to butcher the calf. As I was butchering the buffalo the picture of that slowly moving caravan of Indians kept popping into my mind.

Early the next morning I packed as much of the buffalo on my horse as he could carry. Walking Lance to within a couple hundred yards of the moving band of Indians I stopped and waited. I intended to just drop the meat and ride away, but something seemed to draw me to them.

The young boy obviously was in charge and stopped the caravan with a wave of his hand, coming on alone. I kept my hands in plain sight as he walked up.

I almost fell over when he stopped about twenty feet from me and said in broken English, "Thank you. My name is Slow Turtle."

"My name is Watson," I said.

"We have had no meat for many days. Come, join our camp." With that he turned and walked back to his group, giving instructions as he went. They immediately set up a small camp. They must have been powerfully hungry. As they prepared the meat Slow Turtle and I talked.

"Slow Turtle, how did you learn to speak English?" I asked.

"Many traders stop to trade. Some spend much time."

"What are you doing out here on the prairie with only these old ones?" I questioned.

"Our people move to their winter camp. They move fast. We follow. Chief Iron Eagle bestow great honor on me. It is my responsibility to see that the old ones get there safe."

The honor seemed a bit hard to me, but their ways were not mine and I had much to learn. We gathered buffalo chips to keep the fire going and soon we all sat eating buffalo steaks and stew. The only food they had with them was a few greens and a couple of wild onions. I wondered just how long it had been since they'd eaten solid food.

As they ate the men told stories of their youth, enjoying the food and rest from their travels. The women listened to the tales as though they had never heard them before, but I was sure any one of them could have told the stories as well as the speaker.

Slow Turtle had to translate most of it for they spoke few words that I recognized, but their hand movements told a lot of the story.

When Lone Bear told of the bear with the big hump on its back, attacking him he pulled the smock off his shoulder to show the scars. He said he had to play dead and just lay there while the bear mauled him, until it lost interest and lumbered away.

Red Eagle told of stealing four horses while the Cheyenne sat around their campfire.

And Tall Tree reminisced of the buffalo hunts he had been on when the buffalo outnumbered the leaves on the tree in midsummer.

Sometimes they would run them off a cliff and there the buffalo would pile up ten high at the bottom. There would be much feasting and dancing after such a hunt.

I pulled my coin out and started rolling it up and

down my fingers. That held their interest for quite a while. Each one had to try. Full Moon was the best of them at getting the coin to move and each time it went to another finger she would let out a small giggle.

I picked up three small rocks and started juggling them. At first, they held back thinking this was magic for the rocks seemed to float in midair. Each time I stopped they begged me for more. I entertained them until well after dark and decided to stay with them for a few days for they needed more food for their journey.

In the days that followed I learned much about these people, how they made their clothes, how they hunted, what you could eat, which was poison out here on the prairie. I even learned to speak their language some.

Game was still scarce, but I managed to get a deer the second day out. Each night I would juggle for them, and they would tell stories of their youth.

Seven days out we started to see buffalo on a regular basis. We also saw tracks of other Indians and each time

Slow Turtle would say "Not our people."

I never could tell how he knew it was not his people. Slow Turtle taught me more about tracking in that week than I had learned in my short life.

We all gained by our strange friendship. I could see the old ones moving with more agility as their diet improved and I was learning every day.

The sky was just starting to brighten in the east. I wasn't sure what woke me, but all my senses were alert. I looked over at Slow Turtle. He was sitting up on his blanket and looking around. Lance snorted and I realized he had warned us.

Suddenly they were there. Three of them, charging us with tomahawks in one hand, a knife in the other, yelling a scream that made your blood run cold. I didn't even realize my gun was in my hand until I squeezed the trigger. I fired twice so close together it sounded like one shot. At point blank range a forty-four carries quite a wallop. The brave was in midair when the bullets hit him.

He actually went over backwards. I turned and fired at the second one, not ten feet from me and got the same reaction for my bullets hit him hard, but he tried to get up and come after me. I fired three more times before he went down and stayed down. Slow Turtle had killed the other one with his knife.

It happened so fast I couldn't believe it had happened. The camp was in turmoil, everyone talking and nobody listening. Slow Turtle reached down and took the scalp from the brave he'd killed, and I lost my supper right there. He took the hair from the other two and I made sure I wasn't watching. Slow Turtle was bleeding from his right shoulder where a knife had grazed him.

Little Fawn rummaged through her pack and selected some greens I had seen down by the water. These she pressed on Slow Turtle's wound. I'd have to remember that plant and pick some the next time I saw it. It could come in mighty handy.

We sat around the fire while everyone gave their

version of the attack with me coming out braver with each telling. When Little Fawn finished working on Slow Turtle, we mounted the two horses and backtracked our attackers to their night camp.

It was less than a mile from our camp where we found their horses securely tied to nearby trees. Slow Turtle was a real hero when we trotted back to camp leading three horses. I led the way because Slow Turtle had the scalps tied to his waist and they were slowly dripping blood down his leg, a sight that made me sick each time I looked back.

When we broke camp that afternoon everyone got to ride. That even put a smile on my face, and it'd been a while.

That night we had some old people with sore legs and rumps for they had not straddled a horse for many a year. Again, Little Fawn went to her backpack and brought out plants. Comfrey, I think, was one of them and the other smelled like the camphor oil Ma used to use on us. Little Fawn mashed them up and boiled them in a little water and rubbed it over their sore muscles. I guess it helped.

They weren't complaining the next day.

Around the fire each retold the happenings of the morning. A couple more telling's like these and I wouldn't be able to recognize myself. Heady stuff for a sixteen-year-old.

I juggled for almost an hour and Full Moon held our attention rolling the silver dollar through her fingers as the moon raced across the sky. I made a present of a silver dollar to Full Moon that night and she gave me a large gold nugget from the deerskin bag around her neck in exchange. It was much too valuable for her to give away, but she insisted so I quietly put it away to treasure always.

TEN

Two days later we rode over a small ridge overlooking the winter camp of the Arapaho. There were at least seventy tepees, people moving in all directions and dogs running and barking continuously. I tried to say my goodbyes, but they led me into the encampment surrounded by leaping dogs, screaming children and women jabbering and pointing at our caravan. The men stood back, looking fierce and watching carefully as we passed through the camp.

When they got a look at the horses we were greeted like heroes. Slow Turtle sat a little taller on his horse and even the old ones seemed to suddenly appear younger under the envious eyes of their peers.

Slow Turtle rode straight to the tepee of Chief Iron Eagle. There he dismounted, signed me to get down and proudly walked up to Chief Iron Eagle.

"I bring the old ones, each warrior with his own horse, captured from our enemy the Cheyenne. Their scalps hang from my belt. Jimmy is friend." This Slow Turtle later related to me.

Chief Iron Eagle bid us welcome and invited us into his lodge. In the dim light pelts hung along the taut sides covered with drawings of deer, buffalo, and wild horses.

Slowly I lowered myself to the spot indicated by Slow Turtle, trembling inside as I watched two muscular braves stand guard at the opening. A thousand stories flashed through my mind, men skinned alive, tortured at the stake or tied to ant hills.

Silently I listened as Slow Turtle spoke in the guttural language of his people. There Slow Turtle told of their slow journey following the tribe as their food dwindled and the old ones faltered more and more. Then He Who Floats Stones appeared loaded with buffalo to share. He rode with them, taught them the secret of floating stones, and hunted for them. One morning the horse of He Who Floats Stones warned of danger just as the three Cheyenne came over the rise. Showing the heart of a true warrior He, Who Floats Stones shot the first just as the warrior reached him and then turned and caught another as he was attacking from the left.

Slow Turtle's knife stuck straight and true as the last warrior ran at them with tomahawk raised. Slow Turtle seemed to sit even taller as he related how we backtracked and found the horses.

Chief Iron Eagle listened in silence.

When Slow Turtle ran out of words for his great adventure Chief Iron Eagle rose, looking every inch the leader and stated, "Tonight we celebrate the manhood of Slow Turtle, henceforth to be known as Quick Moving Squirrel and our blood brother He Who Floats Stones."

When Slow Turtle rose, I followed suit and gladly walked out into the clear air. He led me to his tepee set up while we sat with Chief Iron Eagle. There he explained what had transpired and what to expect at the evening ceremony.

As the sun was setting, drums called us to the center of camp, where a huge fire burned. There was much dancing and food. My young eyes took in all the spectacle and pageantry, warriors painted vivid red, green, blue, and yellow with the symbols of nature as their legends presented them. Some wore masks of antelope, deer, buffalo, and the mighty grizzly.

But none outshone Chief Iron Eagle in his headdress of eagle feathers cascading down his back. His chest was covered with a shield of animal bones and colored beads. Symbols of lightning coursed down his arms. Around his neck hung a necklace of the talons of eagles.

The drums changed their tempo and slowly everyone found a seat, crowding to be close to the storytellers. Quick Moving Squirrel stood up and told of his adventure. Elaborating and coloring the story so that we sounded like a mighty band protected by the gods, from fierce, but cowardly enemies of the chosen people. Quick Moving Squirrel called me forward and handed me a coin to roll through my fingers. Amid the sounds of astonishment, I heard the giggles of Full Moon. She would be the center of attention for many moons.

Casually Quick Moving Squirrel chose three rocks from the ground. For all his nonchalance I think he planted them there for effect. I juggled those rocks until my arms tired as the warriors stretched and gaped at the flying missiles. And when I allowed the magic rocks to be passed hand to hand, they babbled like children and needed to be assured they were not bad magic.

Again, the drums, but with a low and powerful tempo, as Chief Iron Eagle stepped to the center of the gathering and began chanting. As the whole tribe picked it up, I felt goosebumps rising and watched Quick Moving Squirrel make his way proudly through the warriors to Chief Iron Eagle's side. With much chanting Chief Iron

Eagle placed a hawk's feather in Quick Moving Squirrel's black shiny hair and hung around his neck a doeskin bag such as I saw Little Fawn wearing.

Proudly my friend Quick Moving Squirrel strode over to me and signaled me to join him. Together we walked to Chief Iron Eagle and presented our left wrists. Luckily Quick Moving Squirrel had explained the ceremony beforehand to me or I might have turned around and run when Chief Iron Eagle pulled out his wicked looking knife and slashed us each across the wrist. He quickly bound our wrists together and held them high in the air. Our blood mingled together as it ran down our arms. I was now a true blood brother of the Arapaho and bound by the laws of the chosen people to Quick Moving Squirrel and all Arapaho across the great prairie.

The days passed swiftly as we fished and told stories. A buffalo hunt was planned. A young boy could find no finer existence. The day of the hunt dawned bright and clear as we rode out of camp full of youth, excitement, and joy of living in a glorious time of green grasses, blue skies and far horizons.

The scouts knew where the buffalo were grazing and took us right to them. It was a full day's ride to the beautiful valley.

There they stood in their shaggy majesty. I had seen a few buffalo but nothing to compare to this. There must have been thousands quietly milling around.

That night around the campfire we planned our strategy. Twenty braves were to stand at one end of the valley and the rest would drive the herd in their direction while trying to down the huge beasts from horseback.

Excitement was high and sleep was hard to come by. We all were up before the sky lightened. I will say one thing about the Arapaho, they are brave and skillful riders, for I saw things that day I still don't believe. One brave jumped from his horse onto the back of a big bull and started hacking with his tomahawk. Some would jab with their lances and be thrown off their horses. One leaped onto a cow and reached down and under and slit its throat with his skinning knife. They all rode right into the herd without hesitation. If their pony stumbled, they would be trampled. I shot a large bull with my pistol. It took all six shots to get him down and then I hurried on to try again. It didn't take the buffalo long to cover the four miles across the valley. The earth seemed to be shaking under their weight as they pounded across the grassland.

They cleared the valley, quiet descended. and the dust settled as we spun our horses around and viewed the scene. Buffalo lay everywhere. With adrenaline still pumping we jumped from our horses, gesturing, and shouting as each tried to describe their feats.

Chief Iron Eagle let us continue for a few minutes and then pointed out that the meat would spoil if we kept this up all day.

Laughing, we hurried to the task. Women rode up with travois and we loaded both meat and skin onto them. It took many hours to butcher all the buffalo and skin them, but the tribe would be well on the way to stocking up for the coming winter. New skins were always needed for the tepees and clothing was always in short supply. The warm buffalo robes were especially prized during the long winter months from the fire.

Back at the main camp squaws would be busy for many days stretching, preparing, and sewing for the months ahead. One afternoon Full Moon shyly approached me and asked me to extend my feet. By now I could talk passably Arapaho and with gestures could make myself understood. She wanted to make me moccasins and needed my measurements. I was thrilled but asked her to teach me how to make them. Together we bent over the skins and outlined my feet. With Full Moon's gentle instructions, I soon had a new set of moccasins, but Full Moon wasn't finished with them. She produced a bag full of stones, colored beads and bones and quickly and expertly sewed symbolic designs on each. As she sewed, she explained each symbol, the red wavy lines for swift passage along the trail, yellow starlike symbols for safe journey and rabbit tails for silent travel. I wore these whenever we walked through camp, but quietly made myself a plain pair to wear in the damp forest. Full Moon's moccasins would be kept for those special occasions, and I needed their confidence. Full Moon beamed with pleasure whenever she saw me strutting across the camp with them on.

During the long, dark wintry days the warriors spent days fashioning fine, curved bows and straight shafts shaped over the fire. Games of chance abound, especially a game using two polished bones, one marked with symbols, the other plain. Sticks were used to keep score. The combatants sat across from each other, skillfully moving the bones from hand to hand, chanting in rhythm. The chanting ceased and the opposite player, with much forethought, indicated the hand he thought held the marked bone. Beaver and muskrat pelts changed hands rapidly, plus jewelry fashioned of feathers, claws, or colored stones. Though Quick Moving Squirrel soon taught me to trap the beaver and muskrat I had little to barter with and usually watched from the sidelines.

Like most of the young braves I preferred the out of doors even when the snow reached our knees, clad in soft deerskin boots laced tightly over the leg coverings. When not hunting or trapping we competed in skills needed to survive. Lances and tomahawks flew through the air at rolling hoops and swinging targets tied in trees. Usually, these contests ended amid much cheering, followed by a general free for all. Bodies flew in all directions and more than once I landed in the partially frozen creek much to the glee of my red companions.

Outside the winds changed from cold penetrating to the cleansing breezes of spring. The young warriors hunted daily, supplementing the bland diet of smoked buffalo steaks with young deer and bird. The squaws added green plants gathered by newly running streams.

Another year had slipped by and too soon I felt the need to move on, searching for that unknown over the next hill. Quick Moving Squirrel and I said our goodbyes in the forest one afternoon. I would miss this quiet young boy who took on the responsibilities of a warrior and never wavered. He was truly a partner to walk the trails with, but our destinies were in different directions. In the years ahead, many nights I warded off the loneliness with thoughts of my Arapaho brother somewhere out on the plains.

Indians love ceremonies and leaving was no exception. Around a ceremonial fire Chief Iron Eagle called me forward. Taking a necklace from his neck; he presented it to the four winds, first strong North, then gentle South, to the East for new dawning's and lastly to the glorious Western sunset. His chanting included the sun and moon and the stars.

At last, turning to me he said, "This will keep you safe, for it is strong medicine. It has the claw of the great humped bear, a feather from the soaring eagle, the tooth of the cougar and the tip of our brother, the gray fox's tail. The claw represents courage, the feather speed. The tooth will carry you on silent feet and the fox's tail will give you wisdom. Go, my brother, and carry the wisdom of the Arapaho with you."

It was with great sorrow the next morning that I left the camp of my friends. Quick Moving Squirrel was like a brother and would be in my thoughts forever. Full Moon gave me a big hug and I could see a trace of a tear in her eye for she knew she would never see me again. She pulled out the silver dollar and rolled it across her fingers. That brought a large smile from me. I looked down at the beautiful moccasins on my feet and signed "love". Lastly, I stood before Chief Iron Eagle, thanked him, and called to the heavens to watch and care for my Arapaho brothers.

As Lance and I rode away I reached in my pocket for the gold nugget. It made me feel better for a part of them would always ride with me. I felt the bear claw around my neck and felt the stronger for having it.

ELEVEN

As I moved west the hills got steeper and the streams swifter and I took up my favorite pastime - fishing. I think Lance was glad to be on the move again. I saw deer on a regular basis and didn't have to ride far afield for game. I set my snares most every night and enjoyed a variety of meat for supper, plus skins for clothing. I was moving southwest now toward Denver. I decided to visit Tim. Besides, I longed to play a few hands of poker at a real table and maybe just walk along the streets and enjoy the bustle of civilization again.

When I first caught sight of the mountains they took my breath away, the snowcapped peaks and purple heights hazy in the distance. And there too, I saw my first elk. I didn't know what it was, but it sure was impressive to the young lad that I was. It was grazing in the valley with the wind coming from it to me and didn't catch my scent. I reached slowly for my glass and sat there watching for several minutes. Its rack was magnificent and looked as though it alone weighed over one hundred pounds.

That day I got my first look at the great humpback bear I'd heard so much about. As I rode through a stand of birch trees swaying in the mountain breeze the sound of breaking twigs off to my left riveted my attention. Quickly I reined Lance behind some large bushes for concealment. There, shouldering large bushes and scrub trees aside came the monstrous bear I'd heard so much about. He swayed from side to side, moving with a shuffling motion, power, and strength in every movement.

Lance wanted nothing to do with him and I agreed, though I observed him through my glass for a while from a safe distance. He came up on his hind legs and sniffed the air, catching a whiff of Lance or me and then lumbered off. I checked to see where he headed and made a wide circle around him, for I wanted no part of him.

Now the deer had large racks and big ears. That night I caught a large rabbit with big back feet. I had heard of the snowshoe, but this was the first one I saw. His coat would make a fine hat for next winter.

I'd watched the mountains get larger and taller each day as I approached them, and the beauty grew with them. It takes a lot to overwhelm a boy of seventeen, but the magnificence of the far away peaks did just that. Now I could see where the tree line stopped. Snow covered the tops of the higher peaks, and the evenings were getting colder as I slowly rode higher each day. There were times I would look down at what seemed to be a thousand feet or more to a lake that reflected like a mirror. The water in the fast-moving streams was so cold it almost hurt your teeth to drink it, but it sure tasted sweet.

As I sat there drinking in the beauty of a distant peak, something moved off to the right. You can look all day and not see anything, but if it moves it sticks out like a sore thumb. It's the movement you catch out of the corner of your eye. I got out my glass and studied the high peak. I saw nothing but was sure something had moved just a moment before. There, it moved again. But where? That mountain looked straight up. I kept my glass steady on the spot for a few minutes and out it came into the open, a beautiful snow-white mountain goat with great curling horns.

As Lance and I wound around the mountain trails I knew I'd gotten my money's worth and then some when I bought Lance for, he was as much at home on these narrow rocky paths as he had been on the flat prairie. I let him have his head and there were times I questioned his judgment. The trail would narrow down to the width of a man and if it ran out, we would have to back out, I wasn't looking forward to that. Sometimes I could see straight down for what seemed like a half mile. Lance took it in stride, not bothered in the least. Finally, the trail widened, and I felt a little better. I came out on the other side of the mountain and surveyed the new country.

There in a meadow far below were brown dots. I put my glass on them and spotted a small herd of elk or deer. At this distance I couldn't be sure which.

Off to the left I picked up something, either dust or smoke. As I studied it, it appeared to be moving, an indication of dust and perhaps a trail. I got out my compass and took a reading, checking the sun to see how much daylight I had left. There wasn't enough left to make it to that trail, so I moved off and found a good campsite for the night.

With my line and hooks in hand I soon found a rushing stream and quickly caught my dinner. This was living, but I felt the urge to mingle again with people. Besides, I was tired of my own cooking.

Later the following day I reached the source of the dust I'd seen the day before. It was a road, not well-traveled. The tracks were plain in heavy dust. A wagon pulled by a brace of six horses had stirred up the dust. The wheel tracks were deep and wide, like a freight wagon would make. Two riders rode with the wagon.

It looked like we were in for a storm this evening as clouds gathered on the high points and I started hunting a campsite early. Denver, if that's what lies ahead, would have to wait for another day. The cloud masses quickly came in with lightning brightening up the sky off to the northwest. I left the road a few minutes later, following a dry gully, scanning the area for a spot that offered shelter for Lance and myself. I found what I was looking for about one mile up the steam bed, a large rock shelf stuck out over the dry gully about ten feet up the bank with a ledge overhead to protect us from the onslaught. I led Lance up and started gathering dry sticks for a fire. Just as I put the last of my coffee on, the wind picked up and it started to sprinkle.

It was raining hard in the mountains, and I enjoyed watching the storm approach. This one was putting on quite a show as the lightning danced from one peak to another. The rain came in torrents as I put a chuck of venison over the fire.

As the venison sizzled, I sat back drinking the last of my coffee, musing of the day past, remembering the good days when Pa and I went hunting along the river. How proud he was when I supplied the turkey for Thanksgiving so long ago. My mind raced with memories of Pa and I training horses, of Jake and my river crossing. I tried to picture Ma and little Becky, but that was so long ago.

Suddenly a noise broke into my reverie, a rumbling sound like nothing I'd ever heard before. As it got louder and louder, I glanced at Lance. He was pawing the ground, obviously upset.

The dry creek bed suddenly flowed with two feet of water, and it was rising. Then I knew what was happening. The sound was deafening as I grabbed my saddle and bags, yelling for Lance to follow. I scrambled up the side of the draw and saw it coming, a wall of water fifteen or twenty feet high, pushing everything in front of it. Logs seemed to fly and tumble up out of the raging turbulent brown water. Even large boulders were pushed along like they were weightless. We'd made it in the nick of time. Supper and my cooking utensils were gone, but it felt good just getting out of there with my life. I stood on the rim looking down at the muddy water for several minutes trying to control my trembling knees.

The rain was letting up as I led Lance into a grove of cedar to set up camp. By the time I got a fire going it was dark and the rain had just about stopped. I stripped off my sodden clothing and hung them on sticks around the fire. Next, I cleaned my guns and wrapped myself in my blankets, thankful they were wrapped in the bedroll and dry.

I had heard cowboys talk of flash floods as we sat around the campfires on the trail drive, but until you experience it yourself there is no way you can imagine the incredible speed and force behind the solid wall of water as it drives through a dry bed.

The next morning the sun was shining bright. My clothes still hung damp on the sticks, and I got a late start as I waited for the morning sun to dry them completely. Damp jeans really chafe. I had the time and I waited. Later I rode by the gully that almost cost me my life and marveled at the placid stream now meandering down the gully less than six inches deep.

TWELVE

We were on the road west to Denver. After the storm the air smelled fresh and the grass sparkled in the sunshine, a brilliant green. It felt good to be alive.

It was late in the evening when I topped a hill and four buildings stood in the narrow valley. I rode my pony up to the saloon, knowing this was a place to gather information. Besides, a beer sounded good.

There were two miners and a cowboy drinking at the bar, from the looks of their clothes. They all sized me up as I walked up to the bar.

"What happened to you, cowboy?" was the greeting I got from the bartender.

I realized I must have looked a mess, my clothes tattered and torn, my hat a misshapen lump clinging to my head.

"I watched a flash flood firsthand." I laughed and

added, "How about a beer?"

The barkeep shook his head and said, "You're in luck, boy. We just brought in a load of ice off the mountain yesterday and the beer's ice cold."

"I lost most of my gear as I hightailed it out of the creek bed." I told them. "Another lesson learned. Is there a place here to pick up supplies?"

The bartender nodded, "Mrs. Jackson, over at the general store, should have everything you need, including a new hat."

I laughed, knowing what a spectacle I made and asked, "How far is it to Denver?"

"About twenty miles down the trail, an easy day's travel," one cowboy spoke up.

I remarked about the deep wagon tracks I'd been following before the storm hit and found they were ore wagons filled with silver headed for the processing mills in Denver.

Lance and I spent the night. In the morning Mrs.

Jackson fixed me up with a coffee pot and skillet, plus coffee and enough supplies to see me to Denver. This depleted my cash, and I rode to Denver with empty pockets.

THIRTEEN

It was shortly after noon when I rode Lance down the main street of Denver. Construction was everywhere. Stores, houses, and warehouses were going up almost like magic. Piles of lumber were stacked in every open spot more than one foot wide. With workmen hammering, toting, and sawing, it smelled of fresh lumber, warm sun and sweat. The noise, after the quiet mountain trails, was deafening. Drovers were swearing at their mules, cracking whips high over the backs of the straining animals. Hammers and saws kept a tempo in the background. Above all of this the mills grinding silver ore rumbled day and night.

I counted five churches under construction. Saloons were everywhere and, like the mines, were open twenty-four hours a day. The general stores were like nothing I'd ever imagined. They were bursting at the seams with anything I could imagine and lots I didn't even know what they were for. There were even stores with ready-made dresses, all frilly, covered with lace and doodads, the likes of which I'd never dreamed of. I stopped and gawked at every store front. There was no question of me being a country boy.

Ladies paraded along the boardwalks in every color imaginable, carrying parasols against the Colorado sun and carefully lifting their skirts as they traversed the dusty streets. Many had bustles stuck out the back. I laughed the first time I saw one, but I did admire their hats sporting birds, long trailing feathers, and lace.

The houses up on the hill were like nothing I'd ever seen, covered with fancy "gingerbread" trimming. I learned they were owned by mine owners and merchants, sometimes changing hands overnight as fortunes were won and lost on the many gambling tables. At that moment I thought of Ma, the log cabin and quiet firelight in the evening.

"No, I didn't want to trade my memories for their large sprawling houses."

The gambling houses drew me like a magnet. I visited one after another, just getting the feel of them again. Money was everywhere with many tables having no limit. It was contagious watching cards flipped across the tables and coins racked in. Reaching in my pockets I realized how broke I was. Traveling across the country, money meant little, but here it was the byword.

First thing in the morning I would have to transfer money to a Denver bank, but first I'd better find a place to stay and get cleaned up.

I had some more surprises coming. They wanted a dollar to keep my horse overnight, two dollars for a room plus fifty cents for a bath. I quickly counted my money and found I was down to six bucks, plus my gold nugget and that I wouldn't part with. After a bath and a hot meal, I was down to three dollars but ready to take on the town.

Lanterns hung on almost every post, lighting the town like day. I picked one of the better gambling houses and walked up to the bar, ordering a beer. I almost choked when the bartender asked for fifty cents. At these prices I would need money in a hurry. All the poker tables were full, with crowds hanging around the higher stake tables. I just blended in and watched.

There were a few professional gamblers, but most were just plain working men looking for a good time and too much money in their pockets. I drifted from one table to another, watching the action. Big money was laying in piles around the dice games, but my game was poker. I longed for the feel of the cards, but my finances said I had to wait a few days, so I headed back to the hotel and a good night's rest.

The bank was crowded the next morning as I walked in. Like every business in Denver, they were doing a booming business. When my turn came, I found it would take ten days for my money to be transferred and verified. Meanwhile they would give me a voucher for fifty dollars to tide me over.

I laughed as I left the bank, knowing fifty dollars in this town would not stretch too far. I headed for my room to pick up my bedroll knowing Lance and I would be spending the next couple days living off the land. I stopped by one of the general stores to pick up some supplies and couldn't resist the canned peaches. They ride heavy, but they sure do taste good. The nights were still cold here in the mountains, so I picked up a new blanket to replace my old one. I liked the feel and color and was told it was made by the Ute Indians that traded in the area.

Lance gave me a short whinny when I entered the livery stable, and I knew he was ready to hit the trail. We headed northwest out of town, meeting two different ore wagons, both with guards riding shotgun and outriders following close behind. I said my "Howdy's" as we passed and all seemed friendly, though I wouldn't want to be on the receiving side of those shotguns.

In the late afternoon I heard a blast up ahead and spurred Lance as I hurried to see if I could help. Smoke was billowing out of the mouth of a mine as I pulled up. Four miners were settling down around a campfire. They laughed as I pulled Lance to a halt and explained my haste. They explained that they set charges to blow the next day's ore loose, letting the mine set overnight in case of cave ins.

"Sit down and have a cup of coffee." they offered.

After digging through my saddlebags for a cup I sat down and learned a bit about mining. Most of the ore had been low grade. There was promise of a high grain vein further along. Twice claim jumpers had tried to attack them, slowing them down. Two stood guard while two worked the mine.

When I told them I was going up the mountain for a week or two they offered me thirty dollars a deer and fifty for an elk, saying it had been a while since they had had fresh meat. I took them up on their offer and accepted the mule to haul back meat.

I spent the night with them, taking a turn at standing guard. We all enjoyed yarning around the fire. I juggled a while and having mastered four stones at a time, kept their attention. Rolling a coin up and down my fingers astonished them for their fingers were stiff with callous and hard work.

By noon the mining road was behind me, and I followed a game trail. It was overgrown and hadn't been used for some time. A small meadow opened before me and there I sat my horse and enjoyed the wonders of nature, a family of beavers hard at work building a dam across a small stream. A stand of aspen on the far side showed the work of these busy fellows. Trees were down all over with beavers dragging them to their site.

I spooked a cougar halfway up the ridge. It literally flew from beneath our feet and hightailed it up the hillside. The mule almost took me and Lance down the mountain as I felt the jerk on the saddle rope and the mule broke the lead rope, bolting down the mountain trail, making noises only a mule can make. I watched the cat bound out of sight before turning Lance to retrieve the mule. It had run about a half mile before it settled down and was munching grass as though nothing had happened.

I shot a grouse for my supper. I was happy when the mule paid no attention to the gunshot. I was seeing signs that elk were in the area and made an early camp. In the morning, I would scout the territory for a large bull. I knew you couldn't eat the horns, but the boy in me sure liked the look of those big antlers. I practiced my fast draw while the fire was taking hold. That grouse sure tasted good, and I topped it off with a can of peaches. As I sat back with my second cup of coffee a pesky squirrel came in close barking and scolding for invading his territory. As the sun went behind the trees the woods came alive with night sounds. Off at a distance a pair of wolves answered each other at steady intervals. The bugle of the bull elk and the scream of the cougar after dark will bring the hair up on the back of your neck as the dark closes in. I loved these sounds, each a part of the great and beautiful country I was riding through. I picketed the mule, but turned Lance loose knowing he would not stray far and would come on the first whistle.

There was frost on the grass as I woke to a clear sky, the sun still behind a peak. The air was clean and brisk as I took in deep breaths. It felt good to be alive as I splashed cold mountain water over my face. The fire started quickly and soon the aroma of fresh coffee filled the air. After mixing up some pan biscuits I sat back and gloried in the wild beauty all around me. Lance, hearing the morning noises of camp, came in on his own.

While finishing breakfast I heard three different bulls bugling. None of them had the deep rasp of a mature bull. I had seven days to kill so there was no hurry.

Checking the mule to make sure it wouldn't stray

far from camp Lance, and I went on one of many scouting trips. The first two days I never saw so much as a cow, though the signs were there. On the third day two young bulls gave me a glimpse of them, but nothing to shoot at. On my way back to camp I spotted a big bull on the other side of a valley. Lance and I worked our way over as quietly as possible, but he was nowhere to be found. We spent several days searching for that bull.

I settled for a young bull on the ninth day and was lucky to get that, for he had been my first shot. I was surprised how much meat there was. It was almost like butchering a cow back home.

And with that thought, a lot of old memories came back.

"Pa, I sure miss you."

I rode back to camp for the mule and returned to pack the meat in the skin and load it on the mule. I stripped the tenderloins out, leaving the head and ribs for the wolves and started back down the mountain to the miners' camp.

It took a while longer to set up camp that night for I had to unload and tie the meat high in a tree to keep it from predators. I cut off a nice chunk of tenderloin for my supper and, believe me, I can't remember eating anything better, except Ma's apple pie.

That night both Lance and the mule stayed close to the fire. Wolves stalked the camp, smelling the fresh kill. I kept the fire going bright most of the night, adding fuel each time the wolves woke me. Their eyes glowed green outside the circle of fire. With first dawning Lance was anxious to break camp and gave me a little nudge.

It was an easy ride to the mine, and we pulled in early in the afternoon, greeted with big smiles when they saw the mule loaded down with meat. They had most of the ore cleared out for the day, so they set charges for the next day and prepared for a big feed.

Around the fire they showed me samples taken that same day, pieces with quite a bit of color and they were sure they would hit it big anytime. I guess that's what keeps them digging - the promise of tomorrow. I built up their fire while they set the charges. We sat around the fire chewing our elk and telling stories. Since I was by far the youngest, I mostly listened.

Two of them had been to California in '49 and talked of the clear blue ocean that stretched as far as a man could see and the tall trees that took three men to reach around.

Jim, the tall miner, went into their lean-to and brought out a nugget about half the size of a small egg, telling us he had picked it up after a flash flood in this area.

I dug out the nugget Full Moon had given me and showed it around.

They asked me to juggle some before we turned in. As I juggled, I told about the ranch, Pa, Ma getting sick and Becky meeting up with that snake. I guess I needed to open up with some friendly folks and rid myself of the cloud that traveled so far west with me.

In the morning, I said my goodbyes and left with a standing invitation to come back anytime and hunt for them. I was to remember these miners and use it to my advantage later, but now my only thoughts were of clean sheets, a soft bed and aces and queens flipping across the green felt tables.

FOURTEEN

It was shortly after noon when I walked Lance down the main street, pulling up in front of the bank, the clanging and banging of the bustling city ringing in my ears. The money was waiting for me, and I withdrew five hundred, heading for a room and stable, to stow my gear, itching to get in a poker game.

I found a boarding house with a barn in back where I could keep Lance close at hand. Mrs. Jordan was a lady in her late thirties with three children helping her to run the place. She'd lost her husband a year earlier in a mining accident and supported herself and the kids. She was pleasant and a very good cook, setting rules in no uncertain terms as I paid her for the first week's rent.

"There will be no girlies in my home. Breakfast at seven, lunch at twelve noon and supper at six. The coffee pot is always on. Please, help yourself." All this in one breath as she led me to my room.

The room was on the third floor with a window facing the street, a bed on one side and a dresser, plus a place to hang your clothes on the other. A small desk and one chair sat in front of the window. I pulled out a deck of cards and played with them for about an hour, just getting the feel of them again. It felt good to sit and shuffle them, practicing all T.J. had taught me. I dealt all fifty-two up, one on top of the other.

Turning the deck over I then called each one before turning it over. I called all fifty-two correctly and repeated that five times just to test my memory, then practiced moving the coin up and down my fingers for another hour before going down to supper. I was as ready for the tables as I'd ever be.

All the high-stake tables were filled as I scanned the big open drinking and gaming room at the Golden Nugget Saloon. Still wearing range clothes, I definitely did not look like money or anyone who knew about cards. By nine a chair opened up at a table I had had an eye on. I casually walked over and watched a couple hands before offering to fill the empty chair.

"Name's Jimmy. Mind if I sit in?" I questioned.

The big man across the table did the talking, "Takes one hundred in chips and pot limit, chairs open. No wild games."

No one offered their name as I bought three hundred in chips. We played dealer's choice, usually seven card stud, five card stud or five card draw, my kind of poker.

They were all drinking pretty heavily, and I had a beer now and then. The money moved around the table for the first couple of hours with me holding my own. But as they kept drinking my pile of chips started growing and by the end of the night, I cashed in almost seven hundred in chips, a profit of four hundred. Not bad for my first night.

I checked my pocket watch and was surprised it was almost three.

I wouldn't make breakfast this day and I'd better tell Mrs. Jordan not to figure me for breakfast for a while.

The next morning, I ambled down about nine and told Mrs. Jordan not to expect me for breakfast until further notice. The mother in her made her frown, but she offered to reduce my rent. I was well satisfied with our original arrangement and would not let her take less. In the months that followed Mrs. Jordan became the mother I so sorely missed and her children, the family I'd lost.

I gambled at night and fished or hunted during the day giving the meat to Mrs. Jordan. It was a nice feeling to again be a part of a family and Joe, the oldest boy, joined me whenever he could talk his mother into it. We tried every stream and scouted for deer, enjoying the freedom and companionship.

I looked up Tim a few days later and found he had

settled right in as a cub reporter and gofer. My money was tucked away in his desk waiting for me to ride in and claim it. Tim spent his time away from running the presses out on the street just talking to people. He would come back to the office, go over his notes and come up with something of interest to the throngs of people passing through Denver. He had learned to set type and run the presses, sometimes working twenty hours a day, and loving every minute of it.

His Dad's partner was a short stocky man in his late forties with no family. Tim became the family he missed, and he happily taught Tim everything he knew about the newspaper business.

Tim and I became good friends and did a lot of hunting and fishing together when Tim had time off and the weather permitted. Tim knew what he wanted in life. I envied him. I was getting quite a reputation at the gambling tables. A kid taking money from old timers was a novelty and for quite a while each new hand in town had to try me, but gradually only the better players sat down. Like all gamblers I had my bad nights but those were few and kept the interest up. My bankroll was growing again, but there were still those hills waiting for me.

It was late summer when we had a nice game going. The cards were running my direction, the night was young, and I was three hundred dollars ahead when a chair opened up and a miner stepped over. He'd been watching the game for about an hour and drinking heavily. I started to protest, but thought better of it. He dumped a sack of gold nuggets on the table worth well over a thousand dollars and bought five hundred in chips. The crowd kept swelling around the table as he held his own for the first half hour, ordering a drink almost every other hand and talking meaner with each drink. I should have seen the trouble coming, but my cards were running good and my pile kept growing. He bought more chips.

The game was five card draw and I opened with

two small pairs, drawing one card. He also took one card, but didn't open, so I figured he drew to a straight or flush. I checked my draw and found I had filled my full house. Betting fifty dollars dropped everyone except the miner, by this time weaving in his chair. He checked his cards and found he had hit his flush and raised me his last two hundred in chips. I called, turning over my full house. He just sat there looking at the cards for a few seconds not believing what he saw.

His chair fell backwards as he leaped to his feet yelling, "You cheat!" and went for his gun.

His gun almost cleared leather when I made my move. My gun seemed to leap in my hand and my aim was true as my bullet hit him hard in the chest. He fell back over the chair, dead. I said not a word as I cashed in my chips and walked out the door.

I lost my supper in the alley next to the Golden Nugget. I'd killed a man and didn't like it. Now I had a reputation I didn't want.

It was shortly after midnight when I climbed the steps to my room. I felt weak in the knees and my stomach was still churning. Killing those two Indians had upset me, but nothing like this. Indians were considered no more than animals, but this had been a hardworking, God fearing, white man. I lay awake a long time before sleep came that night.

I was up early the next morning and headed to the sheriff's office. Sheriff Conway thanked me for stopping by, but told me he had ten witnesses that told him it was self-defense. Sheriff Conway did tell me that the miner's name was Joe Bokovich and had left a wife and two small children living on the outskirts of town. He'd already talked to her this morning and explained the shooting.

I left the sheriff's office feeling worse than ever. I went back to my boarding house and drank two cups of coffee with Mrs. Jordan.

Then I saddled Lance and headed for the Bokovich place, not knowing what I'd say when I got there.

Mrs. Bokovich was much younger than I had expected. I guessed her to be in her early twenties, with a daughter hanging on her skirts, just barely walking, plus a wide-eyed boy not more than six. I introduced myself and wondered what had brought me here.

She invited me in for coffee and we talked a while of Denver, her kids, and the weather. I asked what she would do now. She had no plans, but as we talked, she mentioned a restaurant that was looking for a cook.

I finished my coffee, feeling very uncomfortable as the little boy never took his eyes off me.

I said, "I'm sorry about last night. I can't bring him back, but I can give you what he lost in the game as a stake for the future, if you'll take it. He had no business in that game. He was drinking too much."

She looked at me with tears in her eyes and said, "God bless you. I knew Joe's temper and drinking would get him in trouble one of these days." I left a poke with twelve hundred dollars in gold coins, a small price for a man's life. Yet many lose theirs for less. I felt sorry for those two children that would never know their father, but I realized Mrs. Bokovich would soon remarry, for young widows didn't last long here in the west and she was good looking.

Tim and I had a go around about how and what he would print about the killing. I just wanted it forgotten. There was already enough talk without the paper. Finally, Tim agreed to print "Bokovich was killed after pulling a gun during a card game at the Golden Nugget. He leaves a young wife and two small children." Not a very detailed account, but a big favor to me.

Giving the widow Bokovich the money eased my conscience slightly, but I stayed away from the tables for a few nights. There was a difference when I walked down the boardwalks now. People looked at me a little longer. Talk seemed to die down as I joined a group. I was no longer a kid. Now I was a dangerous man, someone to stay away from, for my gun got faster each time someone repeated the story.

I heard men saying, "He don't look so fast to me, after all that was just a miner, not a gunfighter." and argued whether they might be fast enough to face me.

I spent a lot of time up in my room rolling my coin up and down my fingers and practicing my fast draw, hoping I'd never have to use it again. But as in any growing town after a week it was old news. Still, I made up my mind to move on. I didn't play any more poker for I didn't need the money and I'd lost my taste for it.

Tim taught me how to set up type and run the press. I spent many an hour pushing the handle up and down. Because of my poor spelling Tim would check the type carefully after I set it up. I was learning in a new direction now and enjoying it. The paper came out twice a week and it was always a last-minute rush to get it out on time. My help was greatly appreciated. I began to take an interest in local politics and once or twice was able to give Time a new slant on a feature story. Reading became a pleasure instead of a chore and I found myself often sitting at Mrs. Jordan's reading whatever material came my way.

Fall was fast approaching, and I felt the old itch to see the other side of the hill. I said my goodbyes to Tim, but not before he made me promise to write. Another tie, but not one I'd lose for many a year. I deposited what money I had, keeping a hundred to stake me. I now had over twenty-four thousand dollars, a small fortune. The banker suggested I take a bank voucher with me for a thousand dollars that I could cash at most banks.

The hardest goodbye would be Mrs. Jordan, but I found she had anticipated me. She made me a big sack to take along and added a leather vest she had been making for me. I gave each of the kids a handshake and a silver dollar and then turned to Mrs. Jordan as any son would his mother. She gave me a hug, patted me on the shoulder and pushed me out the door, wiping her eyes on her apron.

I jumped on Lance's back with my eyes mighty

blurred. Riding out I listened to the grind and hammer of the mills, a part of my life and again I was riding away.

Lance was in high spirits and ready to shake the dust of this town. At the edge of town, a man stepped off the boardwalk and called my name. A lad a couple years older than me. I had seen him around town, and he always seemed to have a chip on his shoulder. I reined in Lance and walked over to him.

His coat was open and pushed back, revealing a tied down holster.

"Heard you're leaving town, Mr. Watson."

I hesitated and said, "Sorry, I don't think I know you."

He took up a stance directly in front of me and said, "Name's Johnson, Harold Johnson, and I want your reputation. Killing a miner is one thing, but I want to see how you stack up against a real gunman. Talk is, you're pretty fast with that gun. Climb down off that horse and let's see how fast."

I sat my horse looking down at Harold Johnson for almost a minute before speaking, "Mr. Johnson, I've no quarrel with you and I can't see why you are dead set on getting yourself killed, for if I step down off this horse that's what is going to happen." I could see doubt starting to come into his eyes as I slowly unbuttoned my jacket.

"Mr. Johnson, you've lost no face yet for none can hear this conversation so tip your hat and I'll say goodbye. If not, I'm about to crawl off this horse and you'll be dead in a matter of seconds."

Heavy talk for a young kid, but effective against a coward with nothing but talk to back him up. Harold looked straight into my eyes and saw no fear. He stood there a few seconds, took two steps back and tipped his hat.

I tipped mine, saying, "Goodbye and good luck." He'd need it.

As I rode out of Denver I was filled with relief and couldn't help thinking that next time I probably wouldn't be so lucky. At the same time, I knew I would have beat him and that bothered me.

FIFTEEN

I headed northwest out of Denver into some of the most beautiful country I'd ever seen. Lance felt right at home, so did I. Most of the trails high up had a light dusting of snow and I let Lance pick the trail. I had my doubts on several of those narrow switchbacks, but Lance never failed. We lived off the land and were in no hurry. I'd been told about a place north where water flew straight up a hundred feet in the air and springs ran warm all year long.

This was the land of the bears with the big hump, grizzlies and eagles soared overhead. It stirred the imagination of a young boy and so I moved on in some predestined direction only God knew.

Some days we made quite a few miles. Yet others I could almost look back and see where we'd camped the night before. The fishing was good and game in abundance, so coffee and salt was all I needed from my saddle bags and occasionally flour for pan biscuits. These were leisure days for Lance and me. I figured we'd gone about a hundred miles since leaving Denver. The nights were cold, but the days were brisk and pleasant. Snow lay in patches and ice covered the trail in many places, so travel was slow.

As we came over a ridge Lance shook his head, stopped, and brought his ears forward. I was instantly alert with my gun out and ready. Lance just stood stock still for what seemed like several minutes smelling the air and listening. He began to move at a slow walk and about thirty yards down the trail in a patch of snow was the largest bear track I'd ever seen. I dismounted and studied that track for several minutes judging the weight from the depth of the prints and his enormous stride. My curiosity got the best of me. I wanted to see the animal that fit those tracks.

Lance didn't share my enthusiasm when the bear

left the trail and I had to urge him to follow. The bear was in no hurry, and neither was I. As we rounded the side of the mountain the footing was loose and there suddenly, not fifty feet away he stood waiting for us. He was on all fours, his hump high on his back as he swayed back and forth. I'd heard a lot of tales about the giant bear, but nothing compares to seeing one at close range. The bear watched us for a couple minutes and then came up on his back legs to get a better look and that's when I realized how big this monster was. I could see he was working his nose to catch our scent. He came down on all fours and I started to turn Lance for flight away from this giant when he turned his rump to us and ambled off in a dignified manner. I watched him go and Lance happily started off in the opposite direction.

An uneventful day followed, and we made an early camp next to a beaver pond alive with rainbow trout. I caught about fifteen, keeping the two biggest for supper. Night comes early in the mountains and as soon as the sun goes down so does the temperature. I sat around the fire, wrapped in my blanket, moving a coin up and down my fingers and gazed at the stars. If you haven't seen stars on a clear night in the mountains you've missed a sight to last you for the rest of your life.

I slept.

Lance nudged me with his nose, and I was instantly awake. I sat up in my blanket and reached for my gun, all my senses alert. With his ears straight up Lance was looking down our backtrail. The sun hadn't peeked over the mountain tops yet, but daylight was coming fast. As I slipped on my boots I smelled smoke. There was almost no breeze so all I got was a whiff, enough to tell me I had company. My fire was out. I sat a couple of minutes listening and watching Lance for I was sure he'd hear someone approaching long before I would. I'd come to depend on Lance, knowing he'd saved my bacon several times in the past.

There would be no breakfast this morning for I was

sure a fire down the valley could mean nothing but trouble for me. It was too late in the fall for miners, and I wanted no part of Indians. I covered the burned-out fire and raked it with a bush so that it was noticeable from a distance. Anytime a group of Indians caught a white man alone he could be in trouble, and I wasn't about to stick around to decide if they were friendly.

Finding ground that was hard next to the trail, I urged Lance forward and up the side of the mountain, leaving few tracks. We found a game trail and followed that, keeping a fast pace most of the morning. I pulled some jerky from my saddle bags and ate in the saddle. We made more miles that day than we had in the last four. The next three days we traveled from early morning to late at night, setting up camp in the dark and up by first light, putting distance between me and the Indians. Friendly or not, I wanted no part of them.

It was steady downhill now as we moved out of the mountains and into Wyoming territory. Cheyenne was now my destination, but there were no road signs in the wilderness, and I only knew the general direction. I kept the mountain ridges to my left knowing they would take me in the direction of Cheyenne.

A long two weeks later I came onto a well-traveled road and followed it into town. The sign posted at the edge of town read "Rawlins, Wyoming Population 87." I'd missed Cheyenne by about a hundred miles.

I holed up in Rawlins for about three days getting a badly needed haircut and eating high on the hog, as Pa used to say. While passing the time of day, sitting in what served as saloon, general store and eating establishment I heard again about the spring that blew water a couple hundred feet into the air. It sounded a bit far-fetched, but I had nothing better to do and made up my mind to see this geyser, as they called it.

Lance and I headed northwest. It was mid-September, and the weather was pleasant. By ten in the morning, I could shed my coat, but nights were cold, and my blankets were pulled up around my neck by morning.

About four days out Lance and I stopped early and set up camp by a large lake. I started a fire and hung a small pot of beans over it to simmer while I caught my supper. The coffee was close to the fire so that it would be ready.

I found a comfortable spot with a large oak to lean back on and set back to enjoy the solitude. No more had my worm hit the water when the lake exploded as a fish hit my line, broke the pole in two and was gone and I was standing with half a stick in my hand watching the ripples move across the lake.

All thought of cramped legs and sore muscles fled as I ran for a new pole and bait. It wasn't long to wait for the next strike. As I slowly pulled my line in, I felt a jerk and started tugging in the line as fast as I could. A couple times I had to give line but continued to steadily gain on this fish. This was my first encounter with what they called a pike. It was all teeth and body, long and narrow.

What a grand fight. Just for the fun of it I caught a couple more and threw them back. One was more than I'd eat that night.

As I put the fish in the skillet I glanced up at Lance and saw him perk up, looking at our backtrail. Setting the pan down carefully I stepped back out of sight where I could see the trail. A rider came into sight. About the same time, he must have smelled our smoke and stopped his pony. He located the camp and brought his horse on in, at a slow walk, hailing the camp. Seeing he was alone I stepped out where he could see me.

"If you're friendly, walk your pony on in. There's coffee on and you're welcome."

He walked his pony in, making sure his hands were in plain sight and pulled up about ten feet from me saying, "Name's Walters. Most folks call me Red."

I sized him up as he climbed off his horse and judged him to be about twenty, in need of a haircut and shave. He stood close to six foot. His gun hung low, the rawhide trailing the bottom of his holster where he tied it for a fast draw.

"Bring your coffee cup and plate and set. My name's James Watson. Call me Jimmy."

We shook hands.

He dug in his saddlebags and joined me by the fire with his cup and plate, while I stirred the beans and turned the fish.

"Hope you like fish." I said. "I don't know what I caught, but it's big enough to feed a couple hungry cowboys."

We sat around the fire eating our food and talking. It felt good to have someone to talk to. He was from down in the Arizona territory, mostly desert country and described a canyon as deep as the mountains were high. You could follow it for miles and not find a way to climb down. At the bottom a river raged over rocks. He told of cactus that stood thirty feet high and of a desert that held all the colors of the rainbow and a forest made of rock.

Obviously, he loved that part of the country, and I enjoyed listening to this slow talking man who had seen a part of the country I didn't know existed.

Red related how he got in a shooting scrap.

"It was a fair fight, but this guy has three brothers and a father who is king of the roost, so the best thing I could do was ride. The fight was over a dance hall girl, and it didn't amount to a hill of beans. I had a few drinks. So did the other fella. Our honor was at stake and the next thing guns were drawn. I came out the winner and headed out of town."

I told Red, "I'm heading northwest of here to see a spring that spouts water a couple hundred feet in the air or so I've heard tell. You're welcome to trail along. A lot of people back in Rawlin talked about it and I want a look. They say there's hot springs up there where you can take a bath in the middle of winter, if you've a mind to, and be as warm as toast."

Red listened and slowly spoke, "I'm in no hurry,

but if those brothers are on my backtrail I don't want to buy anyone else trouble."

"Well, Red." I said, "I've got just about the best watchdog you ever did see, in that their horse. If there is any trouble around, he'll let us know, so you might just as well take a ride with me. If they come one at a time it's none of my affair, but if they come all three at once I'll cut myself in for a piece of the action."

I kind of liked this slow talking man from the south and the further we rode the better I liked him. He was a man to cross the river with.

We weren't pushing our ponies. The following day we saw dust on our trail. It looked like more than one rider. Late in the afternoon we topped a ridge and got a good look. They were about two miles back and with the help of my glass I could make out the riders.

It was the three brothers from Arizona. Picking our campsite very carefully that night we took precautions and made sure it was easy to defend if the need arose. We pulled a couple logs about the size of a man into camp and covered them with our saddle blankets, putting our hats on the ends. They lay about fifteen feet from the fire in the shadows.

About seventy feet back of the camp we spread our blankets behind two large rocks. There was good grass close by so I knew Lance would stay close.

Red wasn't much for sleeping that night, but I convinced him that if anything stirred Lance would let us know. We sacked out about ten. The sky was clear, and stars shone brightly as the moon was in its first quarter.

There was little wind, and I was sure Lance would hear them long before they got into camp.

About three hours later Lance gave me a nudge with his soft nose.

I rolled over, touching Red on the shoulder, and whispered, "Something's happening out there."

Lance faced to the south with his ears straight up and I knew someone was sneaking into camp on foot.

When they were within twenty feet of the bedrolls they started blasting away at those logs, until their guns clicked on empty shells.

Then we both stood up. "You boys looking for me?" Red asked.

You could have heard a pin drop, as they all looked up and saw Red and I with our guns pointing at them.

"Boys, you're out of lead, so you better lay them down before Red starts shooting." I commented.

The guns fell like hot potatoes.

I looked over at Red and said, "What do you do with bushwhackers down Arizona way?"

I could see him smile as he stated, "That's a hanging offense down my way."

"That's what I had in mind, Red. But I'd like to wait till morning so I can see them dangle."

I kept my gun on them while Red tied them up, hands and feet. I put the coffee back on for I knew there would be no sleep this night. Red and I drank coffee the rest of the night and came up with a plan we thought was more fitting than a hanging.

First light Lance and I took a ride to their camp and gathered up their belongings, which wasn't too big a chore for they hadn't set up camp and most of their gear was still tied to the saddles on the weary horses. I came into camp trailing the horses behind me. From the look on their faces, they were sure they were about to hang.

We broke camp early loading all their gear onto their horses and untied the three hombres.

"Strip." I said loud and clear.

The big mean one called Leonard spat back, "No two-bit, half-grown kid is going to hang me naked."

That brought a smile to Red's face, and he said, "We had a change of heart overnight. Now get those damn clothes off before we change our minds again."

They started striping and mumbling at the same time but stopped at their long johns.

"Get it all off, right down to your skin unless you'd

rather hang." I snarled.

They finished striping and we put the clothes in their saddlebags. They were a sight to see, three grown men out in the middle of nowhere, naked as a jaybird.

As we climbed into our saddles Leonard said, "You're not going to leave us out here with no horses or boots!"

Red looked him in the eye and queried, "Would you rather hang? The choice is yours. We'll drop your horses off in Cody about seventy miles north of here. I figure a man walking with no boots should make ten miles a day. We'll leave word at the livery to hold them for seven days. If you're not there by then they're his to sell."

"If we ever catch you boys on our backtrail again we shoot on sight."

Red tossed a full canteen to them as we rode off.

Shortly after noon three deer ran across our trail and Red brought down the last one, a small doe. We cut off a hind quarter and strung the rest of it up along the trail, feeling sorry for those three boys back there on foot. We decided to leave a knife so that they could cut the meat off and a small packet of matches. That was the best we could do for them. At least we gave them more of a chance than they had given us when they shot our blankets to pieces.

Then we headed on into Cody. It turned out it was only about fifty miles. They'd have a shorter walk.

SIXTEEN

It was late afternoon as we rode into Cody and headed for the stable. There we explained the situation to the livery man, telling him there should be three footsore, sunburned boys limping in in about four days to pick up their horses. If they didn't show in six days the horses were his.

He laughed fit to be tied," I like your brand of justice. Should be easy to spot, naked as a newborn and twice as red."

With that he went into another fit of laughter. We left him wiping his eyes and grinning ear to ear. That story would be around town in nothing flat.

Our room had a double bed and hot water for a much-needed bath. Feeling spunky we headed for the barber shop. An hour later and ten pounds lighter we stepped into O'Malley's for an Irish dinner, whatever that meant. It was a kind of stew with lots of vegetables and potatoes, plus large slabs of crusty bread for dunking.

Ready for some serious drinking, at the Half Dollar Saloon was our next stop. We had a good time, both of us drinking more than we had a mind to. A dance hall girl had eyes for Red and he wandered off. I eased up to a small poker game and next thing I was filling a chair, enjoying the feel of cards in my hand and the easy camaraderie on a quiet night, a glass of beer and the give and take of a friendly game.

The game broke up early, a little after midnight. I'd won about eighteen dollars, so I figured I'd treat Red to supper before we left tomorrow, but he was nowhere to be found. I made it back to our room. Red never did make it back that night. Sharing a bed with the dance hall girl seemed preferable to waking up next to a beer smelling cowboy.

I treated Red to a big beefsteak that afternoon and

we headed west out of Cody. The Yellowstone, land of the geyser, lay ahead. We trailed through green forest, all virgin timber, tall and straight, reaching for that blue Wyoming sky. The elk serenaded us in the mornings and the wolves and coyotes did the same in the evenings.

I rolled coins every evening before the fire, keeping my fingers limber. Red even gave it a shot and could move that coin with surprising speed, but juggling was beyond him. My laughing didn't help.

The mountains were getting higher as we traveled forward to our destination. Mountain meadows spread before us covered with a rainbow of wildflowers, a memory for those cold winter nights ahead.

The hot springs were there, giving off steam and easing those saddle-sore muscles as we slipped under the water. They smelled of sulfur, but the comfort was worth a little discomfort.

Then we found the mud springs. What an eerie sight, like thick brown soup, boiling over the fire. The heat was intense. We were not able to get within twenty feet of it. The horses shied away, not liking the heat or the smell of minerals escaping into the air as the muddy cauldron bubbled.

We located the geyser the following morning. As we rode forward onto a swamp area in a large clearing a column of water shot straight up about two hundred feet and sprayed the whole area, us included. We pulled back a distance and settled down to wait for another eruption. We decided to set up camp and scout the area, enjoying the great spurts of water as the hours passed.

Even the bear seemed to enjoy it, for we found quite a few tracks in the area and were able to replenish our meat supply with ease. Plenty of food, magnificent scenery, and a friend to share it with. What more could a young boy ask, and so we rode, enjoying the days slowly slipping by.

One quiet evening I mentioned the beating I'd taken in the river town where I'd met Tim. That set Red off. Seems he was quite a fighter and often fought for money behind local saloons. And so began my training. I learned when to fake and when to duck. My right cross even caught Red a couple times unaware. I'd probably get beat up again a time or two, but at least now I knew how to defend myself and wouldn't be totally beaten.

Each night we spared around the fire, covered with sweat and occasionally ending the evening with a free for all wrestle, laughing and cussing until we had to stop for breath.

After two weeks of snow rimmed mountains, crystal cold streams and cool nights around a friendly fire Red and I decided to move on.

"Enough loafing." Red mused, "Time to get back to a warm bunkhouse and a cot to call my own."

We headed into Idaho. As we traveled a particularly treacherous stretch, narrow and rocky, Red took the lead. The trail broadened and we came around a large boulder to find ourselves facing Leonard, Jack and

Bob, the brothers from Arizona Territory, with their rifles pointed straight at us, ours tied in place with rawhide thongs. I saw the flash of a spouting muzzle and Red came over backwards straight at me. Something stung me in the side and at the same time I felt like I was hit in the head with a hammer, tumbling down the side of the mountain.

SEVENTEEN

I woke with the sun in my eyes, covered with briars and hurting badly as I tried to roll over. Reaching up, I felt a gash across my forehead crusted with dried blood and dirt. My gun was still in its holster, the thong holding it in place.

They made one mistake, leaving me alive. I felt the anger growing in me even as I realized the position I was in. The trail was up above me, steep, too steep' for me in my weakened condition. I moved in and out of consciousness, crawling a few feet and then resting, always going up.

Sometime during the cold night, I reached the trail and slept. Lance woke me just as the sun was coming up. My head reeled, less painful than when I awoke at the bottom of the slide, but my side was on fire. Sitting up I peeled away my shredded shirt and examined the wound. A bullet had plowed a furrow just along the beltline.

I mounted Lance and moved forward to find a level spot to camp and care for my wounds. There in the middle of the trail lay Red's horse and a few feet behind him Red. I realized Red's horse had saved my life, rearing as the bullets flew and catching two meant for me.

About twenty feet ahead a mountain stream cascaded over the rocks. Lance and I headed for an overhang close to the stream. There I built a small fire, heating water to cleanse the wound and for some much-needed coffee. Slowly I pulled the torn shirt away from my body and applied hot compresses to my side using the leaves of the alder I found growing nearby as I saw Full Moon use the winter I spent with the Arapaho.

The lump on my head, obviously from my tumble down the side, was receding. After wrapping my side in my last white shirt from riverboat days I leaned back and slowly drank a couple cups of coffee, gaining strength for the task ahead.

A pot of hunters' stew bubbled over the fire as I carried Red to a small gully and loosened a small slide to cover him. I read a few words from the Good Book packed in my saddlebags and later fashioned a crude cross, burning in the words "A MAN TO RIDE THE RIVER WITH." Not original but it expressed how I felt.

Red and I should have hung those buzzards back there when we had the chance. Only scum would shoot a man in his sleep. Next time I would show them no mercy and there would be a next time.

Weak and weaving from fatigue I crawled under my blankets, ate a few spoonful's of stew and dropped into a deep and much needed sleep.

Morning found my head clear and my side throbbing. After cleansing it again this time with gunpowder and whiskey and rewrapping the wound, I threw some chunks of dried meat in boiling water knowing I needed strength to carry out the plans formulated in my mind overnight.

Red's horse lay as he fell, and it took a bit of shoving to strip the saddle and bridle from the stiffening animal. In Red's saddlebags was a letter from a young woman from Prescott, with a picture, a fine-looking woman smiling out at the world. The first town I hit I'd ship Red's things to her. She must be someone special for Red to carry her picture. Red had never mentioned a girl, but we hadn't talked much about our personal life. We discussed the brothers quite a bit and I knew them by name. That was going to be a help for what I had in mind.

I rode until I found the clearing where they had tied their horses and set up the ambush. Studying each track carefully I knew I would recognize them even mingled with others. Slow Turtle had taught me well.

They were in no hurry; sure, no witnesses were left behind. But I needed rest and to let my wounds heal before tackling them. For now, my main objective was to get down off the mountain and into the valley and swamp area where plants grew that the Arapaho used, but now I needed sleep more than anything and time for the wounds to heal.

Slowly and carefully, Lance found his way down the mountain. It was afternoon when I found the valley I was seeking, with running water and skunk cabbage growing close by. Again, I applied hot poultices, consisting of the leaves of the skunk cabbage, to my side to alleviate the swelling. The red angry look was lessening with each application. My strength was coming back, and I'd be able to travel in the morning.

Their trail was easy to follow the next couple days heading toward Jackson Hole, Wyoming. On the third day the skies opened up and drenched Lance and I, wiping out most of the tracks, but I had the general direction.

My side was still too tender to wear my gun belt, but I kept it slung over the saddle horn where it was close at hand and never bothered to put the rawhide thong over the hammer.

Shortly after dark I rode into Jackson Hole and walked straight to the livery stable. Lanterns were burning and inside an old timer forked hay to a couple horses. I ducked my head and rode in.

"Got room for one more?" I asked.

He turned slowly and looked me over, "Two bits a day with hay, four bits with grain, extra two bits if I take care of him. Find a stall and put him in."

I led Lance into a stall, forked in some hay and gave him a generous helping of oats, stripped his saddle and gave him a good rubdown and brushing.

As I brushed, I started a casual conversation, "I'm looking for three boys that might have been through here a couple days ago."

I described the three brothers.

"Missed them. They took off this morning out of town. That will be four bits."

I gave him a silver dollar.

"Keep the change." I said and headed into town.

That put me only one day behind them, so I decided to spend the night. Besides, I needed supplies for what I had in mind. After breakfast the following morning I bought enough food to last about two weeks, plus string and quite a bit of rope for I knew when I caught up with those boys there was going to be a hanging.

I let Lance have his head as we headed out of Jackson Hole. As I rode, I fashioned three small crosses, cutting in the names of each brother. Reaching back in the saddle bags I pulled out the string and cut it in three pieces, tying each into a hangman's noose. Over each cross I tied a noose.

Shortly after noon on the third day out dust appeared about a mile and a half ahead of me. Slowing Lance down so we didn't stir up any dust and give warning we trailed behind. Through a cover of trees, I studied their campsite at sunset, careful not to let the sun reflect off the glass. They had chosen a good site, difficult to sneak up on, but hunting with the Arapahoe had taught me patience and I knew a better opportunity lay ahead.

I broke camp late the next morning giving them a good head start. Lance and I followed at our own pace and three times I studied them with my glass, keeping a safe distance, waiting for dark.

This time they picked a poor camp secure in the knowledge that no one knew of their recent activities. As I sat studying the camp they brought out a bottle and passed it around. This was more than I could have hoped for. It was almost midnight before they turned in and I gave them two more hours. Checking the wind, I slipped on the moccasins Full Moon had given me so long ago. Reaching up I felt the necklace Chief Iron Eagle had given me, the claw of the great hump backed bear, the feather of an eagle, the tooth of the cougar and the tip of the tail of the gray fox. Chief Iron Eagle had said these were great powers and I called on them now.

On silent feet I approached their camp. The breeze

was coming from them to me so the horses should not smell me and give off with a whinny. About fifty feet from camp I could hear snoring, a low rumbling in the quiet night. The two, sawing logs, were surely sound sleepers. There was very little moon, but the stars gave enough light for my purpose. I quickly crept into camp and picked up their hats. Next, I carefully lifted the canteens from their place by the fire, ready for morning, and replaced them with the crosses.

There was water to be found in the area, though it was fairly dry. Without canteens and no hats, by nine o'clock the sun would be doing its job, and I would have three angry cowboys riding down the trail.

I sat; glasses focused on the sleeping men. The first man stirred and got up, walking into the brush. As he stumbled into camp, scratching his head and yawning, Bob, the youngest, rolled over and reached for his hat. Suddenly there was mass confusion and I wished I were closer so that I could hear the cussing. They found the crosses, studied them for a few minutes, not comprehending and finally threw them angrily over the hill. As they stomped around their camp making known their frustrations by each body movement, they found they had no water for coffee. A madder group of cowboys I would never want to meet. After much talking, they saddled up and headed south.

I broke camp and followed. A lot would depend on Lance for I was sure they would set up an ambush. It had been to their advantage the last time but this time I would be ready.

I rode down into their camp and found the crosses. Picking them up I put them in my saddlebags for I wasn't through with them yet. Trying to put distance between me and them, they rode their horses hard, but what time they were picking up they would soon lose looking for water. Lance and I were in no hurry, saving ourselves for another day.

That night they chose a good campsite, easily

defended, low, next to a stream. I set mine up high and built a huge fire so they would be sure to see it. I wanted to worry them. This way they would have to post guards and lose sleep. With the sun beating down on them all day without a hat they should be a surely lot, tired and apt to make mistakes. I got the fire going pretty good and then Lance and I circled around and set up camp ahead of them.

Breaking camp early I moved down the trail about five miles and placed the crosses where they would be sure to be spotted. Now they would know they were being watched but couldn't be sure if I were ahead of them or behind. I liked that.

Up on a high ridge where I could watch and not be seen I hunkered down and waited. I realized I was playing a dangerous game, but the boy in me just couldn't resist the temptation to aggravate them.

About a half mile away from their approach to the crosses, I sat and wished I could have heard what they had to say, for this was a game with me and I was having fun.

I could tell they were confused and worried with this new twist, knowing they were being watched.

Twice they set up ambushes, but Lance spotted the first and a reflection from a gun barrel saved me the second time. By ten the sun was shining bright, and a cold wind blew. I knew it was taking its toll. As I rode, I realized how foolish I'd been to tell them I was after them, for the odds were three to one and how was a boy to handle three grown men, mean to boot. I knew then I should have strung them up that very first night while I had the element of surprise. They would have to be separated, but how, I had no idea. I just knew I could not handle all three at once.

They picked up the Gray River and were following it south. This made it difficult for me for the river twisted and turned and I watched for an ambush behind each turn. I left their trail knowing I could pick it up further south.

LaBarge was little more than a trading post, a large

building, well-stocked with staples in one half of the room and the other half serving as a saloon with sawdust floor. The aroma of fresh coffee mingled with the smell of stale beer. a loft over the bar area with three rooms served overnight travelers. Two drifters leaned on the bar drinking rye whiskey. The owner, a large man, well over three hundred pounds, with a full beard and rolls of fat, showed the easy living he had grown accustomed to behind the bar. I bought a few supplies I needed and a shot of whiskey and rode out for I knew they were not far behind.

Setting up camp on a high ridge I watched everything that moved down there. The barn that served as a stable stood about two hundred feet behind the trading post and from here I had a good view of it. I hoped to get the boys separated in the rooms above, but after checking the building from all sides I found the only entrances were the front and back of the trading post.

It was late in the afternoon when they came riding

in and pulled up to the hitching post. They wearily trudged in, soaking in the shade and liquid. An hour later they came out sporting new hats and canteens as they led their horses to the livery stable. I watched as they carried their saddle bags and bedrolls back to the trading post and knew they would be spending the night. Feeling safety in numbers, I hoped they'd let their guard down.

The sun went down, and lights burned in the saloon. Now I knew what I was going to do.

I broke camp and circled the trading post, coming up behind the livery. Ground tying Lance I crept inside the stable and quickly saddled one of their horses, leading him around back. I slipped on my moccasins and made my way to the back of the trading post. The outhouse stood about seventy feet in back of the saloon and all I had to do was wait for nature to take its course.

Twenty minutes later the back door opened, and I could see Bob, the youngest, outlined in the doorway as he turned to say something to those inside. He slammed the door and ambled back to the outbuilding. As he came out, I hit him over the back of the head with the butt of my pistol. He went down like a sack of potatoes. I pulled his gun from his holster, crammed it in my belt and heaved him up on my shoulder and carried him to the waiting horses. There was little time before he would be missed, but I took time to write a note and tacked it to the stable door.

IF YOU WANT TO BURY YOUR BROTHER HE'LL BE HANGING FIVE MILES SOUTH OF TOWN.

With a little persuasion I convinced Bob to mount the horse when he came to. I tied his hands to the saddle horn and gagged him.

About what I judged to be five miles south of the trading post I found a big old oak tree and threw a loop around a big limb. I had my first hanging. It was clean and quick for I heard Bob's neck snap as the horse ran out from under him.

Now there were two. This was the way of the west. The only law was what you enforced with a rope and a six gun. I left Bob hanging there with his horse tied close by.

EIGHTEEN

So far things were pretty much my way but after the hanging I found myself the hunted instead of the hunter. I was surprised how trail wise they were after I tried several tricks to throw them off and still, they came. Twice they almost boxed me in a canyon, but Lance took a trial more suited for mountain goats than anything else.

For the next several days they pushed hard. I knew it was time to make a stand. I didn't like being the hunted and was afraid they might get a lucky shot off and hit Lance. I needed to choose a spot where I had the advantage.

The next day I spotted a canyon I'd ridden down before. Jack and Leonard were six or seven hundred yards behind me as I started in. I knew the spot I would make my stand. Two hundred yards past a bend there were large boulders and I pulled Lance up behind them, shucking my rifle and dismounting. I took careful aim as they came full gallop around the bend, rushing in for the kill they were sure they had. There was little more than one hundred yards between us when I squeezed the trigger.

The first rider was hit hard as he went over backwards, and the second rider spun his horse around to get cover around the bend. With my glass I recognized Jack laying on the ground. That left Leonard, the meanest of the three. Jack was hit hard, for blood stained the front of his shirt and spread across the ground as he lay on his back where he fell.

Mounting Lance I quickly started down the canyon, keeping close to the walls for cover. Leonard tried a few more shots, but they careened harmlessly off the protruding rocks. The canyon was bisected by several narrow passes leading out in all directions. Lance and I knew our way out and took a rocky trail, leaving no tracks.

The odds now were one on one again. Whether Leonard would be nursing Jack or burying him I had no way of knowing, but it didn't really matter. I'd wait.

Lance needed rest for they had pushed us hard for several days and I had no idea what was ahead. I found a campsite with lots of grass and turned Lance loose while I sat on a high ridge watching the terrain. Twenty-four hours of rest did us both a lot of good and we rode refreshed, back up the canyon to pick up their trail. At their campsite I found a new grave. Now it was two down and one to go.

I could tell from the tracks Leonard was not hunting for me. He was leaving the country, switching horses, and making good time. He wanted out. I lost ground as he'd ride about two hours on one horse and switch to the other. Lance was a good horse with lots of staying power, but I didn't want to push any harder than I was. Leonard made no attempt to cover his trail, heading south as fast as he could.

We headed toward Craig, Colorado. Six days later I rode into Craig and headed for the stables. There, stabled and content was Leonard's horse, plus his brother's. He'd sold them as soon as he reached town. Leonard's horse was a big roan and good for lots of miles. I made inquiries around town and found he'd bought a ticket for Grand Junction, Colorado. The stage made two overnight stops, one at Meeker and one at Rifle before it went on to Grand Junction.

The roan was a good horse for he had spent several days chasing me and I knew that horse had staying power, so I laid out cash for him. I would have a good road all the way following the stagecoach and would make good time.

I rested a day to build up the horses and moved on. Using Leonard's trick, I transferred horses about every two hours, pushing them harder than I really would have liked to, but they were both strong and I knew they could take it. We rode through Meeker, the stage about eight hours ahead of me, without stopping. I got down to Rio

Blanco, picked up a shortcut to Grand Valley that saved me twenty miles and was soon several hours ahead of the stage.

Grand Junction would be where I'd make my play, still about sixty miles south of here. I arrived almost a day ahead of the stage, grained and fed the horses and gave them both good rubdowns. I wandered over to the stage office to check arrival times. It was due in tomorrow around noon, giving me almost twenty hours. I needed the rest.

After checking in at the hotel and taking a badly needed bath I stretched out the bed enjoying the luxury of sheets and the feel of clean clothes against my weary body. Later that evening I walked around the town, found a clean restaurant, and ordered the largest steak on the menu. After making the rounds of the bars I crawled into bed and slept the night through.

Following a good breakfast I relaxed in the barber shop, exchanging gossip. About eleven I walked back to the stable and saddled the roan, bringing him to the stage office where I tied him to their hitching post.

The hardest part was the waiting. I found a place at the saloon across the street with a clear view of the stage stop. The stage was almost two hours late by the time it came rolling in. Two ladies and a drummer got off, then Leonard stepped down. He hadn't spotted the roan yet as he reached for his bag. With the carpet bag and rifle in the same hand he turned toward the hotel and immediately noticed the roan. He stopped dead, then walked over, not understanding how this could be. He put his hand on the roan's front shoulder not believing this could be his horse, but there was no doubting the saddle. He looked at the saloon and made a few steps towards the door, setting his carpet bag and rifle down outside. He squared his shoulders and walked in.

I was standing at the far end of the bar when he came through the doors. It took him a minute to adjust from coming in out of the sunlight. Then he spotted me.

"Step up to the bar, Leonard. I'll buy you a drink," I said and could feel the butterflies in my stomach.

Leonard dragged his feet through the sawdust as he slowly crossed to the bar not understanding how I could possibly be here.

I told the bartender, "Pour my friend a drink, top shelf, for this will be his last."

Someone left the saloon in a hurry, but I scarcely noticed for my eyes were on Leonard.

He found his voice and asked, "How the hell did you get here?" I smiled and quietly said, "You sent me an invitation when you killed Red. Remember! But you made a big mistake that day when neither you nor your brothers trudged down the mountainside to make sure I was dead."

The door of the saloon flew open and the sheriff and his deputy marched in. The deputy carried a shotgun, resting in the crook of his arm.

"What is going on here?" the sheriff demanded.

I casually commented, "You're just in time to witness a shooting. "

"Not in my town." He threw back and walked over, taking both our guns while the deputy kept us covered.

He looked at Leonard and said, "You just came in on the stage.

The stage leaves in two hours. You will be on it."

He led us to the jail saying, "We've worked hard for law and order here and you two boys aren't going to upset it."

Two hours later Leonard was escorted to the stage and out of town. I was held for twenty-four hours. The next day I went directly to the stage office to study the route. It stopped at Delta, then down to Montrose and eventually Drango, all tolled about one hundred eighty miles. I had no idea whether Leonard would stay on the stage or if he had enough money to buy an outfit. That would mean stopping at each stop and checking to see if Leonard got off. This would slow me down. Again, I bought enough supplies to last two weeks, knowing I would not have time to hunt.

With two horses I should make good time, for they had had two days' rest and would be raring to go. Delta was just a stage stop. They changed horses and fed the passengers. No one left the stage. Then it went on to Montrose where it was scheduled for an overnight stop.

There Leonard bought an outfit and headed across the country. No one noticed which direction he headed. The man at the livery described the mare he had sold to Leonard. The pickings were few and the mare didn't have the staying power of the big roan. Now the roan would be a hindrance, so I sold him to the livery stable for a good price. Lance and I would start off after Leonard one more time.

Two miles down the trail I saw tracks leaving the road. It had to be Leonard for there was no reason for a traveler to leave this desolate stretch of road. I called on everything Slow Turtle taught me for the trail was faint where there was any at all. There were miles I wasn't sure if I had lost him. Then I'd find a leaf turned over or a broken twig and occasionally a part of a track. If a man travels, he leaves a track and if you're patient enough you'll find it.

I was closing the gap and the fifth day late in the afternoon I spotted him down in a valley moving at a slow pace, his pony obviously tiring. He hadn't seen me yet and I wanted to keep it that way. As the distance closed between us, I carefully paced Lance, never coming out into the open where he might see me. That evening, I watched as he set up camp and made no fire for myself, wanting complete surprise.

Up the next morning before breakfast, I sauntered into his camp. His back was to me as he bent over the frying pan, flipping bacon around his eggs.

When I said, "Leonard, you won't need that breakfast this morning!" I was within forty feet of him.

"This is the end of the trail."

As he stood and turned, I think I saw relief in his eyes for he had to be as tired of running as I was.

He was faster than I expected. As a matter of fact, I thought he had me beat. Then I felt my gun jump and buck two more times before he fired the first time. He was holding his stomach as he fell, his gun firing harmlessly into the ground. Just like that it was over.

I slowly walked down to my camp, emotionally drained and returned with Lance. There I buried Leonard in a shallow grave, putting a few rocks on top. I said no words over him and left no cross.

His pony was mountain bred and could fend for herself. I untied her and gave her a slap on the rump. With her tail held high she trotted off across the blossoming field, never noticing the pile of rocks that marked the resting place of the last of the brothers.

Now it was time to continue west, to see what was on the other side of the next hill. Me, not yet eighteen and four dead men on my backtrail. What would Ma think if she were alive!

NINETEEN

It was almost two weeks since I'd buried Leonard. I was moving west slowly, worried that winter would overtake me unprepared while I rode enjoying the country. As I rode, I practiced rolling my coin, sometimes juggling rocks or I'd switch to practicing my fast draw, hoping I'd never be tested again. But this was wild country and the only law outside of town was the law of the six-gun.

I remembered the stories told around the campfires. Most of the fast guns had a reputation and were well known. Even without seeing them you could recognize them on sight from the descriptions tossed across the many campfires under the stars. One wore his gun low, while another drew across his body. But the true fast gun always wore just one. Some dressed fancy, but rarely looked for trouble. It just seemed to find them.

There were a few that hired their guns out, but most were loners.

I knew my reputation would be going up and down the trail. The story of the three brothers and the shooting at the gambling hall would make the rounds. It was a reputation I didn't look forward to and it would grow with each telling. Most men in the west didn't ask for their reputations. It just came.

I was always alert now, trusting Lance, for he would see or sense something long before I was aware of it. Several times as his ears perked up a cat would appear stalking our scent and studying her chances or a bear would stand sniffing the air and amble off. I didn't want to corner either of these, charging around a bend in the trail, and I rode with care.

As we topped a ridge overlooking a long, lush valley the aroma of home cooking floating in the crisp clear air stopped me in my tracks. A well-kept ranch lay ahead, and it had been a while since I'd seen as nice a set up. Majestic mountain made a perfect background for the long low ranch house encircled with a welcoming porch on three sides. A fast-running stream curved behind the cabin and followed a dusty road down the long valley. Well, cared for barns sat to the left of the house with adjacent corrals stocked with well-bred horses.

It was supper time, and I was hoping there was enough for a hungry cowboy. Most folks welcomed strangers for they were starved for news from the outside.

I was spotted about halfway down the ridge. A tall man stepped out on the porch, a rifle on his hip.

When I was close enough, I yelled, "Hello."

He answered with a, "If you're friendly, ride your pony in." From the greeting they were expecting trouble, so I rode in at a slow pace, keeping my hands in plain sight.

At the porch smiling, I dismounted saying, "My name's Jimmy Watson. I'm passing through and smelled your cooking."

The rancher held out his hand saying, "The name's

Bill Cook. Sorry about the greeting. We've had a peck of trouble the past few weeks, so we're a bit jumpy."

"I figured as much." I acknowledged with a nod of my head.

"We're just fixing to eat. You're welcome to join us. Wash up around back. I'll have Joey take care of your horse." he said as a young towhead stepped out to join his father.

I thanked him and together Joey and I walked around back leading Lance.

As I opened the back door, I wished I had taken more time, combed my hair and changed my dusty trail worn shirt, for there in that kitchen stood the loveliest creature I had ever seen.

Mr. Cook was introducing me to his wife and son Joey, but all I heard was "My daughter, Linda Sue."

She was the most beautiful girl I'd ever seen. Her hair was almost chestnut, shining like a newly brushed mare and hung nearly to her waist. Her eyes were as blue green as a mountain lake and seemed to twinkle like the stars in the heavens. Her movements were graceful as she glided across the kitchen, setting the table. She was full of life, laughing and joking with Joey. When she smiled at me my heart must have melted, taking my voice with it. Suddenly I had a lot of trouble talking and felt clumsy. Mrs. Cook was asking me to sit down. I swear that girl even affected my hearing. She sat across from me and I couldn't keep my eyes off her.

They all wanted to hear what was happening back east. I wasn't much for passing the time with small talk, but I had two papers that were less than two months old in my saddle bags. When I brought them out, they were reverently put aside to be devoured over coffee after dinner.

I told them I had been living off the land for several weeks now and welcomed a chance to sit around a table and enjoy a home cooked meal with more than Lance for company. I even offered to help Linda Sue with the dishes, but Mrs. Cook would have none of that. Mr. Cook and I took our coffee out on the porch where we could have a long talk and discuss the newspapers now close at hand.

Again, he apologized for the way he met me as I rode in.

"I settled this ranch about ten years ago, the first rancher in this territory and controlled the water rights for about ten thousand acres. About four years ago a Mr. Bryon moved in a big operation and tried to buy us out, offering about twenty cents on the dollar of what this place is worth. I was having none of that. Besides, this is our home, and we love it."

"About this time our troubles started," he continued. "One of my watering holes was poisoned and I lost fifty head of cattle before I could get it fenced off. Last fall two of my haystacks caught fire right out in the open and my herd started dwindling. Two of my hands were beat up in town and quit. Then Joey and I rounded up a hundred head for a small drive. It took us three weeks to get them ready when some cowboys rode in one night, tore down the holding pens and scattered them to hell and back. I had to take out a loan. Bryon found out about it and bought it up from the bank. It's due at the end of September and he plans to foreclose.

I can't prove he's behind any of this and even if I could the only law around here is in town. The sheriff has no jurisdiction out here. It looks like he has me whipped." Mr. Cook gazed off into the distance rubbing the back of his neck like a man with insurmountable problems.

He had been bottling this up for a long time, for usually he was a reticent man, talking little but taking in the conversation around him. Maybe he just felt the need to talk to another man.

The Cooks were special people. There are some you feel comfortable with right away. Mr. Cook took pride in his word and ranch. Even the barns were painted at a time when few bothered.

Mrs. Cook ran the house with a twinkle in her eyes

and a smile for all. Joey and I hit it off. He was the younger brother I never had, following me like a puppy dog. And Linda Sue —!!!

I casually remarked, "If you could use a hand, I wouldn't mind sticking around a few weeks." I didn't bother telling him Linda Sue was most of my reason.

"I appreciate the offer, Jimmy, but I'm not in shape to pay a cowhand right now, for I've no ready cash."

The need to be with people again was strong and we struck a bargain. I would be paid from his next drive, whether he lost the ranch or not.

In the days that followed he showed me the ranch. There were many more cattle than I expected, most of them not branded for he was shorthanded now. The cattle ran wild through the breaks and canyons, wild as deer.

Bryon left the Cooks alone during this time, secure in the knowledge that he had only to wait for the mortgage to come due in the spring and take over the ranch. That made it easier for us. We rode from dawn to dusk, herding cattle, and branding everything that moved. Joey was only ten, but worked along with us, just like a man. That was the way of the west. You grew up fast. I was living proof of that.

As we rode, we talked about our families and after carefully steering the conversation I found that Linda Sue had just turned fifteen, not quite the marrying age, though they did marry young in the west.

I tried to think of a way the Cooks could save their ranch. I wanted to come right out and give them the money for I already felt I was family, but I knew he was too proud to accept it that way. I had to figure out a way he would be glad to take it and not feel obliged. I had no intention of letting them lose the ranch, for I planned to court Linda Sue and if they moved on, I might never see her again.

One night after supper as we sat in the living room discussing the day's progress I mentioned my friend Tim in Denver.

"With the connections he has I'm sure he could get us a contract with the mine owners for the beef, just as I supplied them a while back. By making several small drives each year rather than one big one we'd stand to get a better price and they might even advance the money, money to save the ranch."

The idea had merit and Mr. Cook immediately started making plans. Now he had a reason to continue greeting the cold dawn, as he rode the long, frigid miles, herding the cattle into the lower meadow.

The next morning, I saddled up and rode the twelve miles into town to send a telegram to Tim. I asked the man at the telegraph office to send a boy out to the ranch as soon as I got an answer, leaving a gold piece as payment.

The days slipped by, and I believe Linda Sue was just as interested in me as I was in her. When it came time to dish out dessert, she always gave me the largest piece.

Obviously, the others noticed also. One day Joey remarked, "Hey, how come Jimmy always gets the biggest piece of pie?"

As I ducked my head, concentrating on the pie, I glimpsed Linda Sue's face turn a bright shade of crimson.

Mrs. Cook stepped in and said, "You just eat what's in front of you. There's more of Jimmy to fill."

Two days later a boy brought the answer we were waiting for. I tossed him a silver dollar and thanked him as he rode off. The Cooks crowded around as I tore open the envelope and read the wire.

> TALKED TO OWNERS.
> WANT TO SET UP MEETING.
> ADVANCE OUT OF THE QUESTION.
> TIM

Mr. Cook was a little down after reading the telegram, but knew it was his only chance.

As we sat around the fire that night Mr. Cook brought out his violin and played with strong, sure hands sending a melody drifting into the twilight as outside the snow slowly drifted down. These were good times.

Occasionally we all joined in and sang familiar tunes Mr. Cook drew from the violin tucked carefully under his chin. Linda Sue's clear sweet voice filled the warm cabin with contentment. It made me feel a part of the family, something I hadn't felt for some time.

As we relaxed, I asked about this rancher, Bryan, where he came from, how he managed to finance a ranch and still buy off the Cook's loan.

"He came out about four years ago as I said. No one knows where he came from and he hasn't offered any information, but he bought the Jenkins Place, south of here, for cash and seemed to have lots of money to spread around. His herd has grown about four times as fast as it should, while our cows seem not to be having calves. He ran off Tomson and bought the James place for pennies. About that time, he turned his attention our way and made me his offer. Shortly after that the problems started appearing here. Most of his time is spent in town."

"What about his personal life?" I asked, interested

in the rancher not in debt up to his neck, but with money to spend, expanding without regard to future needs.

"I don't think he's married or if he is, his wife has never been out here. He fools around with one of the dance hall girls at the Golden Palace and plays poker every Friday night, a high-stake game with some of the more prominent merchants and old Doc.

With the words "poker game" I perked up. This was something I knew about.

"This poker game," I asked, "Is it closed or can a stranger sit in?"

"Far as I know all you have to do is show money. Besides, they'd welcome new money."

Now was the time to tell them about T.J. and the summer spent around the green felt tables aboard the riverboats.

With apprehension I began with meeting T.J. there at the livery stable in St. Louis another lifetime ago.

"I spent one whole winter learning to play the game

and made a decent living. My teacher and best friend, T.J. plied the riverboats during the summer, there I joined him, at fifteen, the youngest man to run a table on the river.

Linda Sue was all ears, for I had never talked about my past and they never asked.

As I talked a plan took shape in my mind.

"Mr. Cook," I explained, "I have an idea how you can pay off the mortgage with Bryon's own money. I apologize for asking, but just how much do you owe?"

"Son, the note is seven hundred dollars, a lot of money, but this is no fight of yours."

"Mr. Cook, there were times in Denver when that much and more passed over the tables. Besides, I'd like to see the look on Bryon's face when you pay off the mortgage with his money.

That brought a smile to Mr. Cook's face as he pictured Bryon turning red as he accepted the money, but still he tried to talk me out of it. Finally, after considerable debate we agreed on a ten percent partnership in the ranch for me if I saved the ranch. I had the money to buy up the mortgage, but this was the way Mr. Cook wanted it.

The week passed slowly. I was as excited as a young boy at the candy counter, anticipating the challenge and excitement as the cards swiftly fell and just as fast, the money changed hands. I spent a lot of time rolling my coin up and down limbering up my fingers. In the evenings I'd shuffle a deck and memorize the fall of the cards.

Friday afternoon I had a nice meal with the Cook's. Too excited to wait any longer I saddled Lance and headed into town. I knew I had to put Linda Sue out of my mind for the next twelve hours and call on all T.J. had taught me.

I reached town before the bank closed and dug my voucher out of my saddlebags. There I withdrew a thousand dollars, more than enough to bankroll the card game I had in mind.

It was almost three o'clock as I left the bank with over a thousand dollars in my jeans. I wanted hard cash to put on that table. The game didn't start until about eight, so I looked up a restaurant and ordered the largest steak they had, wanting something in my stomach if required to drink more than I intended. I'd need a clear head.

It was after seven as I casually sauntered into the Golden Palace and ambled up to the bar to order a beer. Making conversation with the barkeep I let it be known I was looking for action at the tables. Noting the money I flashed, he told me of the big game each Friday night and pointed over to the corner table where the chairs were propped, waiting for players.

Around seven thirty Doc tramped in, knocking the dust from his trousers with a wide brimmed Stetson and headed for the bar. The barkeep introduced us as he refilled Doc's glass for the second time in as many minutes.

Doc looked me over and said, "Son, it takes three hundred to buy in."

"No problem." I countered.

"Well, I have no objections, if the rest agree." he obliged.

They started drifting in shortly after Doc and were introduced one by one. Bryon, a tall thin man, with a straight carriage, dressed as a gentleman rancher, was the last to enter. Bryon especially liked the idea of taking money from a kid and no objections were forthcoming as we all sat down.

Their eyes widened as I pulled a pile of double eagles from my pocket to buy chips. Bryon's eyes shone as he saw himself pulling them in. Too Bad. I had no intention of letting that happen.

"Dollar ante, no wild games and no limit." Doc stated.

We played a lot of five card stud, mixed in with seven card stud and five card draw, the way I liked to play. It started slow, seldom a bet of more than ten dollars, with me holding my own, winning a few and learning how each man played his hand.

As they drank more the betting went up. By the second hour I was a couple hundred ahead and the bets were getting higher. I could see it was bothering Bryon who thought he had an easy mark. By ten thirty Mr. Johnson, the owner of Johnson's General Store, had lost four hundred and pushed back his chair saying, "That's enough for me."

Doc was ahead at least two hundred. Wilkenson, the burly smithy, was out a couple hundred and Bryon had to be out over five, for he had bought chips twice since the game started. That put me over eight hundred ahead.

From the time Johnson dipped out the stakes got steeper. Doc was dealing five card stud, and I had a king up. I made a small bet. Everyone stayed and the second time around he paired me up, giving me a pair of kings. I hadn't looked at my hole card yet and kept the bet small to keep everyone in. When the last card was dealt Bryon got an ace. I looked at my hole card, my third king. I glanced across the table at Bryon. He was the only one that could beat what I was showing if he had an ace in the hole. I loved it and hoped he had the ace. This was the hand I'd been waiting for.

I checked my kings, and he took the bait, making a foolish bet of three hundred. I called and turned over the third king.

Bryon swore, turned red around the ears, and hollered for a drink. Old Doc snickered, irritating Bryon all the more.

"Gimme three hundred chips. We're here to play poker, aren't we!" snarled Bryon.

Wilkenson, a regular Friday night player, expertly shuffled the deck and quickly dealt the next hand. For the next half hour money exchanged hands rapidly with Wilkinson building a fair pile.

The excess liquor and overheated pride was showing as Bryon carelessly shuffled the deck. The cards were falling in the same rotation as the last two hands.

With a deuce and two sevens showing, Bryon bet heavy, and I figured him for a seven in the hold. I needed the queen of diamonds to fill a king high straight flush and if the cards followed the sequence of the last hand the lady was sitting on the roost with a seven behind.

Doc was high and bet, "Ten dollars on my pair of aces."

"Raise you fifty." Bryon countered, as he pushed the chips forward.

I had to get Doc to drop out so that Bryon would be dealt the fourth seven and quickly raised five hundred on the come. Doc folded. Looking over my hand Bryon knew he had me beat going in. He had about two hundred and fifty sitting in front of him and called for another five hundred in chips, cleaning out his wallet. Bryon called my raise and dealt the cards. When the queen of diamonds fell in front of me the smug look left his face, followed by a sneer as the seven dropped in front of him. He figured me for either a straight or a flush and four sevens beat either one. The odds of a straight flush are unbelievable, and he counted out two hundred and seventy-eight dollars, all he had on the table. I called and raised him seven hundred.

He looked at me and said, "I'm cleaned out, but I'm good for it. Will you take my I.O.U.?"

I smiled and said, "It would be my pleasure, Mr. Bryon." He turned over his fourth seven and reached for the pot.

"Not so fast, Mr. Bryon. Where I come from a straight flush beats four of a kind," and turned over the ten of diamonds.

He could have killed me right there. I pulled in my chips, stood up and stretched. "Thanks, boys. Bryon, I'll meet you at the bank at ten tomorrow." and walked over to the bar to cash in my chips, almost three thousand dollars and more than two of that was Bryon's. I gave the bartender fifty bucks and told him to buy the house a drink and keep the change.

The ride back to the ranch was like a dream. I

wanted to win so badly, and it turned out better than I could have hoped for. The light was still on at the ranch though it was nearly three in the morning and the door opened as I rode up. It took me about five minutes to take care of Lance and Mrs. Cook was pouring coffee for Mr. Cook and Linda Sue as I hurried in the back door.

Almost word for word I went over the evening, ending with the appointment with Bryon at the bank in the morning. Linda Sue and Joey had been busy counting the money from my saddle bags and had it stacked in neat piles on the table.

"If I counted right there's three thousand seven hundred eighty-six dollars." Linda Sue exclaimed, practically jumping up and down in her chair.

I started with a little over a thousand and Mr. Bryon still owes me seven hundred." I added. "That makes my winnings around thirty-four hundred. Not bad for one night's work."

Mr. Cook laughed, "When you buy into a man's

trouble you buy in all the way. We'd better get some sleep if we have to be in town by ten."

It was a little after six as we left that morning and headed for town, too excited to be tired. I could tell Mr. Cook was a little nervous about this meeting with Bryon, but I was looking forward to it. I really didn't expect trouble for he didn't know what was coming, but I checked my gun anyway.

Bryon was right on time as he walked through the doors of the bank. We were waiting inside.

He looked at me and growled, "What the hell is Cook doing here?" I couldn't help but smile as I answered, "He just wants to pay off his mortgage that you hold on his ranch."

"What kind of bullshit are you trying to hand me?"

"All we want is a clear deed to the ranch, Bryon." I snapped back.

"Listen Watson, I don't know what your game is and where do you get this "we" business?"

"I've been staying out at the Cook ranch for the past several months and he offered me ten percent ownership if I could save the ranch." I informed him. "So, from now on you deal with both of us. Just get the deed out. There's been enough talk."

Bryon turned and went over to the teller, anger in every step and withdrew the seven hundred he owed me, handing it over with reluctance. I reached in my pocket and dug out fourteen dollars, adding that to what he gave me.

This should cover the mortgage and the interest due." I drawled as I handed him the money.

He didn't want to take it, but with everyone in the bank watching our little scene he had no choice.

The banker drew up the necessary papers and witnessed the signatures.

Bryon glared at me with enough hate in his eyes to kill and snarled, "Watson, you haven't heard the last of this. Tomorrow I'm sending my lawyer out with a fair offer and if you know what's good for you, you'll both sign it."

As Bryon turned to storm out of the bank the boy in me couldn't resist. Mr. Bryon!" I snapped.

He turned and I flipped him a ten-dollar gold piece saying, "It's been a pleasure doing business with you."

In one movement Bryon scooped up the gold piece and threw it at me losing his temper and stomped out of the bank.

I opened an account with my thousand dollars and had Mr. Cook deposit the twenty-seven hundred in his account for working capital on the ranch. He tried to argue with me, but I pointed out that I was now part owner.

As we left the bank Cook remarked, "I think we got ourselves a peck of trouble. Bryon will stop at nothing to get the water rights we control. What he's done in the past will seem like kid stuff. We'd better watch our back side."

The next day Bryon sent two men out to the ranch

with an offer for the ranch. The offer was for about ten cents on the dollar of what it was actually worth. But it didn't really matter what they offered. We weren't selling.

The tall man in city clothes was obviously a lawyer, the other, a hard man with the looks of a hired gun. The lawyer handed me a contract and watched as I struck a match to it.

Out of the corner of my eye I studied the other man, knowing his job was to kill me if we turned down the offer. He stepped down off his horse and started walking toward me. We were about twenty feet away and he looked into my eyes. My eyes were cold and hid no fear.

Right about then he realized who I was. My reputation had caught up with me as he stammered, "My god, you're that Watson, the one from Wyoming."

He was in too deep and didn't know how to get out. I could tell he wanted out. Idly, I wondered how many men they were saying I killed up and down the trail, for most of the stories grew with each telling. This gunman was used to scaring farmers. I'll say one thing for him. He was game, for now he knew he couldn't win.

He was slow, all bluff and I had time to place my bullet. His gun hadn't cleared leather when I felt mine jerk. My bullet hit him in the shoulder, and it hit bone. He would live, but I doubted that that arm would ever be much use to him again.

Mr. Cook stared at me and realized I wasn't the inexperienced young boy I appeared to be. But he asked no questions. This would be one more notch on a reputation I didn't want.

Not so with Joey. He was jumping up and down. "Did you see that! Did you see that! Would you teach me? How many men have you killed?"

Mrs. Cook tactfully interrupted and led him into the house with the gunslinger where she stopped the bleeding and bandaged his shoulder. Linda Sue's hands were shaking as she reached for the broom and swept an already clean porch. Her head was down, and I couldn't see her eyes. Darn, how could I explain killing four men to her!

As the lawyer mounted up, I told him, "Tell Bryon I will be coming into town soon to talk with him."

TWENTY

The following Friday I rode into town for one more conversation with Mr. Bryon. It was after nine when I pushed through the doors of the Golden Palace. Putting both hands stiff armed on the table I leaned across and spoke directly to him.

"If you send any more of your hired guns out to the ranch and if the Cooks so much as stub a toe, I will hold you personally responsible and I will surely kill you."

Bryon just stared at me, hate glowing in his eyes, but cowardice staying his hand.

From the way the cowboys at the bar avoided meeting my eyes, I knew my reputation had made the rounds and in a way I was glad. They would think twice before they tackled me now. I walked up to the bar and ordered a beer. Lifting my glass to Bryon, I downed it in one swallow, turned and walked out.

I walked down to the telegraph office and got off a wire to Tim, describing Bryon and suggesting that he might have a military background from the way he carried himself. Any information Tim could scrape up would be appreciated, I wrote.

During the next couple weeks, we hired four hands to help with the branding, preparing for the spring drive. Bryon had not made his move, though I was sure he was planning something.

Either Mr. Cook or myself, needed to go to Denver to set up a meeting with the owners of the mines and sign the contracts, but I was afraid to leave the ranch unprotected and Mr. Cook didn't want to leave his family.

Nothing was said about the gunslinger, but the game of nerves was telling on me, when at last a young boy from town rode in with an answer from Tim:

FROM DESCRIPTION - ARMY THINKS
BRYON IS WILLIAM BRAINARD,
DESERTER, EMBEZZLER, MURDERER.

ARMY SENDING TWO OFFICERS TO
INVESTIGATE. SHOULD BE THERE IN FOUR
DAYS.
     TIM

The boy was bursting with news from town and said Doc had paid him extra to ride like the wind to reach me. "Johnny Slage is in town and looking for you, Mr. Watson."

I did some quick figuring. The military should arrive on Friday. Flipping the boy two bits, I asked him to deliver a message to Mr. Slage. "Tell Mr. Slage I'll see him on Friday. It will be my pleasure to meet with him."

With that the boy jumped on his horse and rode for town, excited with his small part in the shoot-out between Johnny and me.

Mr. Cook came up behind me and asked, "Who is this, Johnny Slage?"

Around the campfires Red had mentioned witnessing a shooting involving Slage. Slage hailed from around Tombstone or Tuscon, Red's stomping grounds, and Red knew his reputation well. I could almost hear Red in his low, slow drawl reminiscing of earlier times. Slage was small, standing about five feet two and no more than a hundred forty-five pounds, dressed entirely in black with silver snaps on his shirt. Even his boots were black and matched his hat, banded in silver. Red stated that Slage was the fastest draw he'd ever seen, but not accurate. In the shoot-out Red watched Slage get off four shells before the other man cleared leather, but only one hit its mark, even though they were only thirty feet apart. I remembered one of the boys on the cattle drive had said the same thing.

If I could get him to draw at fifty or sixty feet, I felt I would have an even chance for I was good at hitting what I aimed at and was pretty fast myself.

During the next few days, the Cooks tried to talk me out of riding to town, but I'd sent my word and in the west your word was the most valuable thing you owned. There was no way I would go back on mine. Linda Sue barely spoke to me, marching from the house to the well and back like I wasn't there. That hurt, but I knew of no other way to handle the situation. The day I found her crying behind the stable tore my insides and I wanted to hold her close and tell her everything would be alright, but before I reached her, she turned and ran into the house.

I left the daily workings of the ranch to Mr. Cook and the new hands, instead practiced my draw, and worked my fingers around the coin. If there was another way out of this, I couldn't think of it, unless Slage left town and I doubted that. From the stories I'd heard he was one of the few who enjoyed his reputation and added to it when given the opportunity. Bryon must have paid dearly for I heard he came high.

Friday came swiftly and the Cooks insisted on coming to town with me. I would have rather they didn't, especially Linda Sue, but she would have it no other way. We took the buggy, arriving just about noon. The sheriff met us at the edge of town, not approving, but afraid to brace Slage or me. All he asked was that I give him time to clear the street. In answer to my query, he said the stage was due around two.

He carried a double-barreled shotgun saying, "If you insist on going through with this, I can be sure that it's a fair shooting."

Knowing my back would be covered eased my mind. Bryon was not above hiring a rifle to back up Slage, just in case.

Slage was in the saloon waiting for me. I sent Joey to tell him I was in town, and he could open the ball out here in the street at his leisure. I wasn't about to go into his lair.

Slage ambled out of the saloon, followed by Bryon and two of his hired guns. The three of them pulled up chairs as Slage stepped into the street.

I turned to Mr. Cook and the sheriff and more calmly than I felt said, "Keep those boys off my back. This is between me and Slage."

The sheriff casually walked up the boardwalk and leaned on a post about ten feet from Bryon, making a show of checking his gun. The meaning was clear. No interference.

I stepped out to the middle of the street and checked the sun. Directly overhead, it would not be a factor for either of us. When Slage was within sixty feet of me I found my voice and managed to say, "That's close enough. One more step and I draw." and I reached up to touch my necklace once more.

I could tell he didn't like it, but he stopped.

I asked, "What's Bryon paying you?"

I got no answer and added, "I don't know what it is, but it's not nearly enough to die for."

We drew almost as one. He was fast, the fastest draw I'd ever seen and before I cleared leather, I knew he had me beat. I saw the flame from his gun twice before mine jerked and something tugged at my right shoulder.

My gun jerked three more times before my arm went numb and I felt the gun slip from my hand. I was on my knees in the dust and heard Bryon cuss as he and his boys rose and turned into the saloon, leaving Slage laying dead, face down in the street.

I was hit and hurt badly, but Linda Sue was by my side crying and helping me to my feet. With Mr. Cook on one side and Linda Sue on the other they helped me to Doc's office.

There old Doc tore my last white shirt and muttered, "Oh, you'll live to take another pot from me." As he worked, he said, "It's not serious, but you'll never draw like that again. The muscle is torn."

In a way that was good for the reputation of killing Slage would have spread across the country like wildfire. Now my reputation as a fast gun would die there on the street with Slage.

Doc finished patching me up and we walked out of his office just as the stage pulled in. When two men in uniform stepped down from the stage we moved forward and introduced ourselves, leading the way to the sheriff's office.

Major Collins, the ranking officer, handed around a poster of the man they knew as William Brainard. Unless Bryon had a twin brother there was no doubt. With our confirmation the sheriff, Major Collins and Lieutenant Crown left the jail and headed for the saloon.

Lieutenant Collins quickly slipped down the alley and went in the back door as the sheriff and Major Collins marched through the swinging door, going directly to Bryon. Bryon looked up in surprise, assessed the situation and never said a word as they led him out.

TWENTY-ONE

Though my arm was still in a sling, two weeks later we stepped onto a stage headed for Denver, all five of us, Mr. and Mrs. Cook, Linda Sue, Joey, and me. There we'd set up contracts with the mine owners and enjoy the sights of Denver. Joey bounced from one seat to another until Mrs. Cook had to reprimand him, finally relenting, and let him ride up top with the driver.

Linda Sue fussed with her hair, pulling it first over her right shoulder, then up on her head and worried that her dress was too blue, not dressy enough or perhaps she should have worn her shawl. I thought she was the prettiest gal this side of the Rockies, needing neither lace nor fancy doodads and I couldn't wait to step off the coach with her on my arm and introduce her to Tim.

Tim was all smiles as he met us at the stage office.

Following the instructions in my telegram he had reservations at the Denver Hotel and a carriage waiting to carry us through the bustling streets.

After washing off the dust of the stagecoach Tim led us to a restaurant that had us gawking and squirming on our red velvet seats. Candles flickered above our heads, reflecting off hundreds of shimmering spheres of glass hanging from the towering ceiling. Mirrors covered the walls, reproducing the scene in splendid color. Even Joey was awed and unusually quiet as plates of fresh green vegetables, browning meats and potatoes in thick gravy moved across the table to be replaced with heavy cream and fresh fruits beyond my descriptions, plus pastries that melted in your mouth.

Tim called for the bill, but I intercepted it saying, "You have no idea how much you have helped us the past few months. This dinner's on me."

As we got up from the table Tim motioned me aside, "I'm sure the Cooks are tired after their long and dusty journey and would like to rest. Besides, I've got another surprise for you, if they will let you go."

They did and Tim and I started off, both talking and no one listening. I had really missed him. He was mysterious and jumping with excitement as we turned in at the Silver Slipper.

"Have you taken up gambling." I asked, surprised at the surroundings.

"You'll see." was all he would say.

Low and behold, dealing stud at one of the tables was the fanciest vest that I'd ever seen and grinning ear to ear was T.J. Our reunion broke up the game and T.J. got another dealer to fill in for him as the three of us set off for some serious drinking and a lot of catching up.

My first question to Tim was, "How did you know T.J and I were friends?"

Tim grinned and said, "Don't forget, I'm a news reporter and a good one. I make it my business to know things."

We all laughed. I made T.J. and Tim promise to have dinner with the Cooks the next day and T.J. 's comment was, "I wouldn't miss it for the world. Heck, there's no girl as pretty as you say Linda Sue is."

The next morning, I met the Cooks for breakfast and told them about meeting T.J., the man who taught me to draw, to shoot and play poker. He was a pretty special person in my life, and I wanted them to meet him. They were all looking forward to the meal as much as I.

After breakfast I begged off one more time saying I had one more person in town I wanted to look up. We made arrangements to meet at the Silver Spur for lunch.

I looked up the rooming house where I'd lived that summer in Denver for, I wanted to see Mrs. Jordan one more time. The house looked a little shabbier, but warm and welcoming. I knocked on the door and she opened it, gasped, and welcomed me with open arms and a big kiss. We chatted over coffee for about two hours as I filled her in on my life since I left Denver. I told her I had promised the Cooks to meet them for lunch and asked her if she could find her way clear to come join us.

T.J. Tim and the Cooks were already seated as I proudly led Mrs. Jordan into the dining room on my arm and introduced her around. The next two hours were filled with more talking than eating.

Surrounded by the people who meant the most to me I sat in happy contentment, willing the day to last forever. Too soon Tim checked his watch saying, "It's almost time to meet with the mine owners."

The meeting turned out to be a boon not only to us, but the mine owners also. We got a better price, and they saved money from what they had been paying.

Tim's dry comment was, "Not a great story, but it will fill space." Mrs. Cook and Linda Sue were having the time of their lives, for with the contracts signed Mr. Cook gave them a free hand to go shopping. Bolts of soft blue, fresh green and lively yellows tumbled over the chairs and tables in their sitting room. When I laughed as Linda Sue pranced in with a blue hat covered with net and a yellow bird perched on top, she stamped her foot in anger, and I laughed until my sides hurt.

With three more days left before we returned to the ranch, I had to find out one more thing. I spent the next three nights playing poker with T.J. Was the student as good as the teacher! We had a lot of fun, both more or less setting traps, but neither falling into them. T.J. wound up with more chips than I, so he announced himself champ and I had to agree with him, but I told him I'd be back to try again.

We left Denver loaded with bags and boxes. The last thing I did was to close my account at the Denver bank. They gave me a voucher for almost fifteen thousand dollars.

I smiled and thought, "T.J., you might be the champ, but the student's not too shabby."

It was nice to get back to the ranch and open spaces. The hired hands really took hold and showed they would ride for the brand.

Lance neighed with pleasure as I saddled him. He'd been neglected for several weeks and loved the attention I was showing him. I'd removed the sling, but my arm felt stiff, and Doc told me it would probably stay that way.

Up on Lance the urge to see over the next hill was coming back. Lance seemed to sense it and I could tell he was ready if I was.

The Cooks tried their best to talk me out of leaving. I could see the hurt in Linda Sue's eyes for she could not understand how I could tell her I loved her and be ready to ride away. I made a promise to be back before she came of marrying age.

She looked up smiling, "They marry young in the west." I told her I'd be back, bringing a red calico dress to wear at the church social, but the Pacific Ocean was still out there just over the hill, maybe the last hill I would have to look behind.

As I mounted my saddle bags packed by the capable

and loving hands of Mrs. Cook, I noticed tears in her gray eyes and Linda Sue just stood off by herself. I stepped down from my horse and kissed her right on the lips, in front of Mr. and Mrs. Cook! I jumped back on Lance and headed west.

EPILOGUE

Allison and the Model A turned in the drive and the children ran to greet her as she stepped out, her red dress bright against the blue sky. Allison reminded me of Linda Sue so very much, so full of life. Without a doubt she was my favorite grandchild.

Allison hurried the children back up to the giant oak where I sat and kissed me on the cheek saying, "I'm sorry I'm so late, Grandpa, but I just couldn't find a hat to go with my new outfit."

She spun around showing off the pretty red print with a white bow at the neck.

"I hope the children didn't wear you out with their questions." She laughed as she reached into her bag for a yellow yoyo for Bill, some paper dolls for Sue and Old Mack tobacco for me.

Bill jumped up and down and quickly related,

"Grandpa has been telling us all about when he was a young boy, Mommy. He even shot an Indian!"

I treasured these moments with my great grandchildren for it seemed I was always too busy as our children grew up. The kids ran ahead as Allison took my arm and walked slowly up to the main house, reminding me, "You've got just about an hour before Daddy comes in from the upper fields for supper."

The memories wore me out and I headed to my room to take a nap before supper. I passed the old Winchester hanging over the fireplace as visions of Jack coming around the bend of that canyon so many years ago flipped across my mind.

I slowly walked into our room and picked up the old tintype of Linda Sue in her red calico dress and me, taken shortly after our wedding, a tear trickled down my cheek. I'd lost Linda Sue almost a year ago, but I still had all the memories.

As I looked out the bedroom window at the fields

of corn and wheat, I remembered the days those same fields held nothing but cattle. Now there were four barns, two silos, a Model A and two tractors on shiny steel wheels. How times had changed.

Remembering the day like it was yesterday I envisioned the ranch as I topped that ridge and saw smoke rising from the chimney and hoped they had grub for a hungry cowboy.

I walked over to the chest and brought out the gun and holster, the bullet hole still in the belt where either Leonard or one of his brothers had put it. I reached around my waist. Well, things had changed. It wouldn't fit around my belly. I guess I had too much easy living these past few years. Allison's voice brought me back to the present as she called, "Grandpa, supper's ready."

As I started down the steps for supper I wondered if there was still a hill I hadn't looked behind.

THE END

About The Author

GENE WILSON grew up in the rolling hills of southern Ohio. He spent his childhood hunting, fishing, hiking, and taking care of his family farm. After high school he came north to work for Ford Motor Company. There he met the love of his life Judy. He enlisted in the U.S. Army when his best friend was drafted and became a rocket specialist. His passions were poker, fishing for pike, horseshoes and his "O" Gauge model trains which took over most of the basement. He loved his two children, spending time with his grandchildren and everyone he met was soon a close friend. As a long reader of westerns, he always dreamed of adding "published writer" to his list of accomplishments and with the help of my wife, daughter, and granddaughter it has finally happened.

Made in the USA
Middletown, DE
15 April 2024

53058195R00142